Praise for *Nothing Gold Can Stay*

"A gorgeous, brutal writer."   —Richard Price

"Ron Rash is a writer of both the darkly beautiful and the sadly true . . . one of our very finest novelists."   —Richard Russo,
Pulitzer Prize–winning author of *Empire Falls*

"A collection of short stories about Appalachia that are actually more like diamonds: cold, glittering, valuable."
—*New York Magazine*

"A lovely, essential new collection of stories . . . lyrical and honest, grounded in place yet sweeping in scope. . . . [Rash's] prose is elegant, suggestive, and Hardyesque."   —*Boston Globe*

"In his new collection of stories, Ron Rash stunningly renders his native Appalachia as an exotic planetoid governed by its own peculiar orbital laws. . . . Rash is a fast-rising superstar in the North Carolina literary constellation that includes such luminaries as Michael Parker, Clyde Edgerton and Philip Gerard."
—*Charlotte Observer*

"[Rash's] starkly beautiful prose has mapped the heart and soul of southern Appalachia in a way few writers of his generation can match. . . . A splendid new collection . . . shimmering, liquid poetry."   —*Atlanta Journal-Constitution*

"*Nothing Gold Can Stay* is a gripping collection, raw and real, that solidifies Rash as a powerful and imaginative storyteller."
—*Kansas City Star*

"Masterfully crafted. The best of Rash's stories, written in a spare prose style, has an aching lyricism as he chronicles the hard times and hard fall of his characters. The best of the best will haunt the reader long after they're done."
—Washington Independent Review of Books

"The stories of *Nothing Gold Can Stay* are tough-minded, surprising, illuminating even when Rash leaves much unsaid (often the reader comprehends more than the characters can). But no matter when they are set or who they concern, these stories are kin to each other."   —*Miami Herald*

"[Rash] bears comparison to the world's truly great story writers—particularly Nathaniel Hawthorne for the gothic horrors that lie in the human heart and Anton Chekhov for his unflinching eye and his ability to capture a character in a single gesture."   —*Richmond Times-Dispatch*

"Each of the stories in this collection comes to life under the power of Rash's muscular way with words.... The author creates a slice of life so authentic you can hear the rushing water and see the falling tear."   —*St. Louis Post-Dispatch*

"Violence-streaked stories that comprise another fine collection from [Ron] Rash.... His oneness with the region and its people makes an indelible impression."
                                    —*Kirkus Reviews* (starred review)

"Rash's short stories thematically paint Appalachia not as a definitive place but as a series of many interconnected ways of relating to human and environmental frailty. Another fine addition to the Rash bibliography, and a great entry point for the uninitiated reader."   —*Library Journal*

"Rash impresses with clear-eyed, sympathetic writing about flawed and troubled characters."   —*Publishers Weekly*

"A wonderful collection."   —*Booklist*

"Rash's unforgettable, beautifully crafted, sure and strong stories tap into what human beings want from each other, and want from the world."   —*The Independent* (UK)

NOTHING GOLD CAN STAY

Stories

RON RASH

ecco

An Imprint of HarperCollinsPublishers

NOTHING GOLD CAN STAY. Copyright © 2013 by Ron Rash. All rights reserved. Printed in the United States of America. No part of this book may be used or reproduced in any manner whatsoever without written permission except in the case of brief quotations embodied in critical articles and reviews. For information address HarperCollins Publishers, 10 East 53rd Street, New York, NY 10022.

HarperCollins books may be purchased for educational, business, or sales promotional use. For information please e-mail the Special Markets Department at SPsales@harpercollins.com

A hardcover edition of this book was published in 2013 by Ecco, an imprint of HarperCollins Publishers.

FIRST ECCO PAPERBACK EDITION PUBLISHED 2014.

Designed by Greg Mortimer

Library of Congress Cataloging-in-Publication Data has been applied for.

ISBN 978-0-06-220272-7

14 15 16 17 18   OV/RRD   10 9 8 7 6 5 4 3 2 1

Grateful acknowledgment is made to the publications in which the following stories appeared: "The Trusty" in *The New Yorker;* "Something Rich and Strange" in *Shade 2004;* "Cherokee" in *Ecotone;* "Twenty-Six Days" in the *Washington Post;* "A Sort of Miracle" in *Ecotone;* "Those Who Are Dead Are Only Now Forgiven" in *The Warwick Review* (England); "The Dowry" and "The Woman at the Pond" in *The Southern Review;* "Night Hawks" in *Grist;* "Three A.M. and the Stars Were Out" in *Our State* magazine; and "Where the Map Ends" in *The Atlantic.*

For Robert Morgan

CONTENTS

I

II

III

PART

I

The Trusty

They had been moving up the road a week without seeing another farmhouse, and the nearest well, at least the nearest the owner would let Sinkler use, was half a mile back. What had been a trusty sluff job was now as onerous as swinging a Kaiser blade or shoveling out ditches. As soon as he'd hauled the buckets back to the cage truck it was time to go again. He asked Vickery if someone could spell him and the bull guard smiled and said that Sinkler could always strap on a pair of leg irons and grab a handle. "Bolick just killed a rattlesnake in them weeds yonder," the bull guard said. "I bet he'd square a trade with you." When Sinkler asked if come morning he could walk ahead to search for another well, Vickery's lips tightened, but he nodded.

The next day, Sinkler took the metal buckets and walked until he found a farmhouse. It was no closer than the other, even a bit farther, but worth padding the hoof a few extra steps. The well he'd been using belonged to a hunchbacked widow. The woman who appeared in this doorway wore her hair in a similar tight bun and draped herself in the same sort of flour-cloth dress, but she looked to be in her mid-twenties, like Sinkler. Two weeks would pass before they got beyond this farmhouse, perhaps another two weeks before the next well. Plenty of time to quench a different kind of thirst. As he entered the yard, the woman looked past the barn to a field where a man and his draft horse were plowing. The woman gave a brisk whistle and the farmer paused and looked their way. Sinkler stopped beside the well but did not set the buckets down.

"What you want," the woman said, not so much a question as a demand.

"Water," Sinkler answered. "We've got a chain gang working on the road."

"I'd have reckoned you to bring water with you."

"Not enough for ten men all day."

The woman looked out at the field again. Her husband watched but did not unloop the rein from around his neck. The woman stepped onto the six nailed-together planks that looked more like a raft than a porch. Firewood was stacked on one side, and closer to the door an axe leaned between a shovel and a hoe. She let her eyes settle on the axe long

4

enough to make sure he noticed it. Sinkler saw now that she was younger than he'd thought, maybe eighteen, at most twenty, more girl than woman.

"How come you not to have chains on you?"

"I'm a trusty," Sinkler said, smiling. "A prisoner, but one that can be trusted."

"And all you want is water?"

Sinkler thought of several possible answers.

"That's what they sent me for."

"I don't reckon there to be any money in it for us?" the girl asked.

"No, just gratitude from a bunch of thirsty men, and especially me for not having to haul it so far."

"I'll have to ask my man," she said. "Stay here in the yard."

For a moment he thought she might take the axe with her. As she walked into the field, Sinkler studied the house, which was no bigger than a fishing shack. The dwelling appeared to have been built in the previous century. The door opened with a latch, not a knob, and no glass filled the window frames. Sinkler stepped closer to the entrance and saw two ladder-back chairs and a small table set on a puncheon floor. Sinkler wondered if these apple-knockers had heard they were supposed to be getting a new deal.

"You can use the well," the girl said when she returned, "but he said you need to forget one of them pails here next time you come asking for water."

Worth it, he figured, even if Vickery took the money out of Sinkler's own pocket, especially with no sign up ahead of another farmhouse. It would be a half-dollar at most, easily made up with one slick deal in a poker game. He nodded and went to the well, sent the rusty bucket down into the dark. The girl went up on the porch but didn't go inside.

"What you in prison for?"

"Thinking a bank manager wouldn't notice his teller slipping a few bills in his pocket."

"Whereabouts?"

"Raleigh."

"I ain't never been past Asheville," the girl said. "How long you in for?"

"Five years. I've done sixteen months."

Sinkler raised the bucket, water leaking from the bottom as he transferred its contents. The girl stayed on the porch, making sure that all he took was water.

"You lived here long?"

"Me and Chet been here a year," the girl said. "I grew up across the ridge yonder."

"You two live alone, do you?"

"We do," the girl said, "but there's a rifle just inside the door and I know how to bead it."

"I'm sure you do," Sinkler said. "You mind telling me your name, just so I'll know what to call you?"

"Lucy Sorrels."

He waited to see if she'd ask his.

"Mine's Sinkler," he said when she didn't.

He filled the second bucket but made no move to leave, instead looking around at the trees and mountains as if just noticing them. Then he smiled and gave a slight nod.

"Must get lonely being out so far from everything," Sinkler said. "At least, I would think so."

"And I'd think them men to be getting thirsty," Lucy Sorrels said.

"Probably," he agreed, surprised at her smarts in turning his words back on him. "But I'll return soon to brighten your day."

"When you planning to leave one of them pails?" she asked.

"Last trip before quitting time."

She nodded and went into the shack.

"The rope broke," he told Vickery as the prisoners piled into the truck at quitting time.

The guard looked not so much skeptical as aggrieved that Sinkler thought him fool enough to believe it. Vickery answered that if Sinkler thought he'd lightened his load he was mistaken. It'd be easy enough to find another bucket, maybe one that could hold an extra gallon. Sinkler shrugged and lifted himself into the cage truck, found a place on the metal bench among the sweating convicts. He'd won over the other guards with cigarettes and small loans, that and his mush talk, but not Vickery, who'd argued that making Sinkler a trusty would only give him a head start when he tried to escape.

The bull guard was right about that. Sinkler had more than fifty dollars in poker winnings now, plenty enough cash to get him across the Mississippi and finally shed himself of the whole damn region. He'd grown up in Montgomery, but when the law got too interested in his comings and goings he'd gone north to Knoxville and then west to Memphis before recrossing Tennessee on his way to Raleigh. Sinkler's talents had led him to establishments where his sleight of hand needed no deck of cards. With a decent suit, clean fingernails, and buffed shoes, he'd walk into a business and be greeted as a solid citizen. Tell a story about being in town because of an ailing mother and you were the cat's pajamas. They'd take the Help Wanted sign out of the window and pretty much replace it with Help Yourself. Sinkler remembered the afternoon in Memphis when he had stood by the river after grifting a clothing store of forty dollars in two months. Keep heading west or turn back east—that was the choice. He'd flipped a silver dollar to decide, a rare moment when he'd trusted his life purely to luck.

This time he'd cross the river, start in Kansas City or St. Louis. He'd work the stores and cafés and newsstands and anywhere else with a till or a cash register. Except for a bank. Crooked as bankers were, Sinkler should have realized how quickly they'd recognize him as one of their own. No, he'd not make that mistake again.

That night, when the stockade lights were snuffed, he lay in his bunk and thought about Lucy Sorrels. A year and a half had passed since he'd been with a woman. After that long, almost any female would make the sap rise. There was nothing about her face to hold a man's attention, but curves tightened the right parts of her dress. Nice legs too. Each trip to the well that day, he had tried to make small talk. She had given him the icy mitts, but he had weeks yet to warm her up. It was only on the last haul that the husband had come in from his field. He'd barely responded to Sinkler's "how do you do's" and "much obliged's." He looked to be around forty and Sinkler suspected that part of his terseness was due to a younger man being around his wife. After a few moments, the farmer had nodded at the pail in Sinkler's left hand. "You'll be leaving that, right?" When Sinkler said yes, the husband told Lucy to switch it with the leaky well bucket, then walked into the barn.

Two days passed before Lucy asked if he'd ever thought of trying to escape.

"Of course," Sinkler answered. "Have you?"

She looked at him in a way that he could not read.

"How come you ain't done it, then? They let you roam near anywhere you want, and you ain't got shackles."

"Maybe I enjoy the free room and board," Sinkler answered. He turned a thumb toward his stripes. "Nice duds too. They even let you change them out every Sunday."

"I don't think I could stand it," Lucy said. "Being locked up so long and knowing I still had nigh on four years."

He checked her lips for the slightest upward curve of a smile, but it wasn't there.

"Yeah," Sinkler said, taking a step closer. "You don't seem the sort to stand being locked up. I'd think a young gal pretty as you would want to see more of the world."

"How come you ain't done it?" she asked again, and brushed some loose wisps of hair behind her ear.

"Maybe the same reason as you," Sinkler said. "It's not like you can get whisked away from here. I haven't seen more than a couple of cars and trucks on this road, and those driving them know there's prisoners about. They wouldn't be fool enough to pick up a stranger. Haven't seen a lot of train tracks either."

"Anybody ever try?" Lucy asked.

"Yeah, two weeks ago. Fellow ran that morning and the bloodhounds had him grabbing sky by dark. All he got for his trouble was a bunch of tick bites and briar scratches. That and another year added to his sentence."

For the first time since she'd gone to fetch her husband, Lucy stepped off the porch and put some distance between her and the door. The rifle and axe too, which meant that she was starting to trust him at least a little. She stood in the yard and looked up at an eave, where black insects hovered around clots of dried mud.

"Them dirt daubers is a nuisance," Lucy said. "I knock their nests down and they build them back the next day."

"I'd guess them to be about the only thing that wants to stay around here, don't you think?"

"You've got a saucy way of talking," she said.

"You don't seem to mind it too much," Sinkler answered, and nodded toward the field. "An older fellow like that usually keeps a close eye on a pretty young wife, but he must be the trusting sort, or is it he just figures he's got you corralled in?"

He lifted the full buckets and stepped close enough to the barn not to be seen from the field. "You don't have to stand so far from me, Lucy Sorrels. I don't bite."

She didn't move toward him but she didn't go back to the porch, either.

"If you was to escape, where would you go?"

"Might depend on who was going with me," Sinkler answered. "What kind of place would you like to visit?"

"Like you'd just up and take me along. I'd likely that about as much as them daubers flying me out of here."

"No, I'd need to get to know my traveling partner better," Sinkler said. "Make sure she really cared about me. That way she wouldn't take a notion to turn me in."

"You mean for the reward money?"

Sinkler laughed.

"You've got to be a high cloud to have a reward put on you, darling. They'd not even bother to put my mug in a post office, which is fine by me. Buy my train ticket and I'd be across the Mississippi in two days. Matter of fact, I've got money enough saved to buy two tickets."

"Enough for two tickets?" she asked.

"I do indeed."

Lucy looked at her bare feet, placed one atop the other as a shy child might. She set both feet back on the ground and looked up.

"Why come you to think a person would turn you in if there ain't no reward?"

"Bad conscience—which is why I've got to be sure my companion doesn't have one." Sinkler smiled. "Like I said, you don't have to stand so far away. We could even step into the barn for a few minutes."

Lucy looked toward the field and let her gaze linger long enough that he thought she just might do it.

"I have chores to get done," she said and went into the shack.

Sinkler headed back down the road, thinking things out. By the time he set the sloshing buckets beside the prison truck, he'd figured a way to get Lucy Sorrels's dress raised with more than just sweet talk. He'd tell her there was an extra set of truck keys in a guard's front desk he could steal. Once the guards were distracted, he'd jump in the truck, pick her up, head straight to Asheville, and catch the first train out. It was a damn good story, one Sinkler himself might have believed if he didn't know that all the extra truck keys were locked inside a thousand-pound Mosler safe.

When he entered the yard the next morning, Lucy came to the well but stayed on the opposite side. Like a skittish dog, Sinkler thought, and imagined holding out a pack of gum or a candy bar to bring her the rest of the way. She wore the same dress as always, but her hair was unpinned and fell across her shoulders. It was blonder and curlier than he'd supposed. Set free for him, Sinkler knew. A cool, steady breeze gave the air an early-autumn feel and helped round the curves beneath the muslin.

"Your hair being down like that—it looks good," he said. "I bet that's the way you wear it in bed."

She didn't blush. Sinkler worked the crank and the well bucket descended into the earth. Once both his buckets were filled, he laid out his plan.

"You don't much cotton to my idea?" he asked when she didn't respond. "I bet you're thinking we'd have to get past them guards with shotguns but we won't. I'll wait until the chain gang's working up above here. Do it like that and we'll have clear sailing all the way down to Asheville."

"There's an easier way," Lucy said quietly, "one where you don't need the truck, nor even a road."

"I never figured you to be the know-all on prison escapes."

"There's a trail on the yon side of that ridge," Lucy said, nodding past the field. "You can follow it all the way to Asheville."

"Asheville's at least thirty miles from here."

"That's by the road. It's no more than eight if you cut through the gap. You just got to know the right trails."

"Which I don't."

"I do," she said. "I've done it in three hours easy."

For a few moments, Sinkler didn't say anything. It was as though the key he'd been imagining had suddenly appeared in his hand. He left the buckets where they were and stepped closer to the barn. When he gestured Lucy closer, she came. He settled an arm around her waist and felt her yield to him. Her lips opened to his and she did not resist when his free hand cupped a breast. To touch a woman after so long made him feather-legged. A bead of sweat trickled down his brow as she pressed her body closer and settled a hand on his thigh. Only when Sinkler tried to lead her into the barn did Lucy resist.

"He can't see us from down there."

"It ain't just that," Lucy said. "My bleed time's started."

Sinkler felt so rabbity that he told her he didn't care.

"There'd be a mess and he'd know the why of it."

He felt frustration simmer into anger. Sinkler tried to step away but Lucy pulled him back, pressed her face into his chest.

"If we was far away it wouldn't matter. I hate it here. He cusses me near every day and won't let me go nowhere. When he's drunk, he fetches his rifle and swears he's going to shoot me."

"It's all right," Sinkler said, and patted her shoulder.

She let go of him slowly. The only sound was a clucking chicken and the breeze tinking the well bucket against the narrow stone wellhead.

"All you and me have to do is get on that train in Asheville," Lucy said, "and not him nor the law can catch us. I know where he keeps his money. I'll get it if you ain't got enough."

He met her eyes, then looked past her. The sun was higher now, angled in over the mountaintops, and the new well bucket winked silver as it swayed. Sinkler lifted his gaze to the cloudless sky. It would be another hot, dry, miserable day and he'd be out in it. At quitting time, he'd go back and wash up with water dingy enough to clog a strainer, eat what would gag a hog, then at nine o'clock set his head on a grimy pillow. Three and a half more years. Sinkler studied the ridgeline, found the gap that would lead to Asheville.

"I've got money," he told Lucy. "It's the getting to where I can spend it that's been the problem."

That night as he lay in his bunk, Sinkler pondered the plan. An hour would pass before anyone started looking for him, and even then they'd search first along the road. As far out as the prisoners were working, it'd take at least four hours to get the bloodhounds on his trail, and by the time the dogs tracked him to Asheville he'd be on a train. It could be months, or never, until such a chance came again. But the suddenness of the opportunity unsettled him. He should take a couple of days, think it out. The grit in the gears would be Lucy. Giving her the slip in Asheville would be nigh impossible, so he'd be with her until the next stop, probably Knoxville or Raleigh. Which could be all for the better. A hotel room and a bottle of bootleg whiskey and they'd have them a high old time. He could sneak out early morning while she slept. If she took what her husband had hidden, she'd have enough for a new start, and another reason not to drop a dime and phone the police.

Of course, many a convict would simply wait until trail's end, then let a good-sized rock take care of it, lift what money she had, and be on his way. Traveling with a girl that young was a risk. She might say or do something to make a bluecoat suspicious. Or, waking up to find him gone, put the law on him just for spite.

The next morning, the men loaded up and drove to where they'd quit the day before. They weren't far from the farmhouse now, only a few hundred yards. As he carried the buckets up the road, Sinkler realized that if Lucy knew the trail, then the husband did too. The guards would see the farmer in the field and tell him who they were looking for. How long after that would he find out that she was gone? It might be just minutes before the husband went to check. But only if the guards were looking in that direction. When the time came, he'd tell Vickery this well was low and the farmer wouldn't let him use it anymore, so he had to go back down the road to the widow's. He could walk in that direction and then cut into the woods and circle back.

Sinkler was already drawing water when Lucy came out. Primping for him, he knew, her hair unpinned and freshly combed, curtaining a necklace with a heart-shaped locket. She smelled good too, a bright and clean smell like honeysuckle. In the distance, the husband was strapped to his horse, the tandem trudging endlessly across the field. From what Sinkler had seen, the man worked as hard as the road crews and had about as much to show for it. Twenty years older and too much of a gink to realize what Lucy understood at eighteen. Sinkler stepped closer to the barn and she raised her mouth to his, found his tongue with her tongue.

"I been thirsting for that all last night and this morning," Lucy said when she broke off the kiss. "That's what it's like—a thirsting. Chet ain't never been able to stanch it, but you can."

She laid her head against his chest and held him tight. Feeling the desperation of her embrace, Sinkler knew that she'd risk her life to help him get away, help them get away. But a girl her age could turn quick as a weather vane. He set his hands on her shoulders and gently but firmly pushed her back enough to meet her eyes.

"You ain't just playing some make-believe with me, because if you are it's time to quit."

"I'll leave this second if you got need to," Lucy said. "I'll go get his money right now. I counted it this morning when he left. It's near seven dollars. That's enough, ain't it, at least to get us tickets?"

"You've never rode a train, have you?" Sinkler asked.

"No."

"It costs more than that."

"How much more?"

"Closer to five each," Sinkler said, "just to get to Knoxville or Raleigh."

She touched the locket.

"This is a pass-me-down from my momma. It's pure silver and we could sell it."

Sinkler slipped a hand under the locket, inspected it with the feigned attentiveness of a jeweler.

"And all this time I thought you had a heart of gold, Lucy Sorrels," Sinkler said, and smiled as he let the locket slide off his palm. "No, darling. You keep it around your pretty neck. I got plenty for tickets, and maybe something extra for a shiny bracelet to go with that necklace."

"Then I want to go tomorrow," Lucy said, and moved closer to him. "My bleed time is near over."

Sinkler smelled the honeysuckle and desire swamped

him. He tried to clear his mind and come up with reasons to delay but none came.

"We'll leave in the morning," Sinkler said.

"All right," she said, touching him a moment longer before removing her hand.

"We'll have to travel light."

"I don't mind that," Lucy said. "It ain't like I got piddling anyway."

"Can you get me one of his shirts and some pants?"

Lucy nodded.

"Don't pack any of it until tomorrow morning when he's in the field," Sinkler said.

"Where are we going?" she asked. "I mean, for good?"

"Where do you want to go?"

"I was notioning California. They say it's like paradise out there."

"That'll do me just fine," Sinkler said, then grinned. "That's just where an angel like you belongs."

The next morning, he told Vickery that the Sorrelses' well was going dry and he'd have to backtrack to the other one. "That'll be almost a mile jaunt for you," Vickery said, and shook his head in mock sympathy. Sinkler walked until he was out of sight. He found himself a marker, a big oak with a trunk cracked by lightning, then stepped over the ditch and entered the woods. He set the buckets by a rotting stump, close enough to the oak tree to be easily found if something went wrong. Because Sinkler knew that, when it came time to lay down or fold, Lucy might still think twice about trusting someone she'd hardly known two weeks, and a convict at that. Or the husband might notice a little thing like Lucy not gathering eggs or not putting a kettle on for supper, things Sinkler should have warned her to do.

Sinkler stayed close to the road, and soon heard the clink of leg chains and the rasp of shovels gathering dirt. Glimpses of black and white caught his eye as he made his way past. The sounds of the chain gang faded, and not long after that the trees thinned, the barn's gray planking filling the gaps. Sinkler did not enter the yard. Lucy stood just inside the farmhouse door. He studied the shack for any hint that the farmer had found out. But all was as it had been, clothing pinned on the wire between two trees, cracked corn spilled on the ground for the chickens, the axe still on the porch beside the hoe. He angled around the barn until he could see the field. The farmer was there, hitched to the horse and plow. Sinkler called her name and Lucy stepped out on the porch. She wore the same muslin dress and carried a knotted bedsheet in her hand. When she got to the woods, Lucy opened the bedsheet and removed a shirt and what was little more than two flaps of tied leather.

"Go over by the well and put these brogans on," Lucy said. "It's a way to fool them hounds."

"We need to get going," Sinkler said.

"It'll just take a minute."

He did what she asked, checking the field to make sure that the farmer wasn't looking in their direction.

"Keep your shoes in your hand," Lucy said, and walked toward Sinkler with the shirt.

When she was close, Lucy got on her knees and rubbed the shirt cloth over the ground, all the way to his feet. Smart of her, Sinkler had to admit, though it was an apple-knocker kind of smart.

"Walk over to the other side of the barn," she told him, scrubbing the ground as she followed.

She motioned him to stay put and retrieved the bed-sheet.

"This way," she said, and led him down the slanted ground and into the woods.

"You expect me to wear these all the way to Asheville?" Sinkler said after the flapping leather almost tripped him.

"No, just up to the ridge."

They stayed in the woods and along the field's far edge and then climbed the ridge. At the top Sinkler took off the brogans and looked back through the trees and saw the square of plowed soil, now no bigger than a barn door. The farmer was still there.

Lucy untied the bedsheet and handed him the pants and shirt. He took off his stripes and hid them behind a tree. Briefly, Sinkler thought about taking a little longer before he dressed, suggesting to Lucy that the bedsheet might have another use. Just a few more hours, he reminded himself, you'll be safe for sure and rolling with her in a big soft bed. The chambray shirt wasn't a bad fit, but the denim pants hung loose on his hips. Every few steps, Sinkler had to hitch them back up. The bedsheet held nothing more and Lucy stuffed it in a rock crevice.

"You bring that money?" he asked.

"You claimed us not to need it," Lucy said, a harshness in her voice he'd not heard before. "You weren't trifling with me about having money for the train tickets, were you?"

"No, darling, and plenty enough to buy you that bracelet and a real dress instead of that flour sack you got on. Stick with me and you'll ride the cushions."

They moved down the ridge through a thicket of rhododendron, the ground so aslant that in a couple of places he'd have tumbled if he hadn't watched how Lucy did it, front foot sideways and leaning backward. At the bottom, the trail forked. Lucy nodded to the left. The land continued downhill, then curved and leveled out. After a while, the path snaked into the undergrowth and Sinkler knew that without Lucy he'd be completely lost. You're doing as much for her as she for you, he reminded himself, and thought again about what another convict might do, what he'd known all along he couldn't do. When others had brought a derringer or Arkansas toothpick to card games, Sinkler arrived empty-handed, because either one could take its owner straight to the morgue or to prison. He'd always made a show of slapping his pockets and opening his coat at such gatherings. "I'll not hurt anything but a fellow's wallet," he'd say. Men had been killed twice in his presence, but he'd never had a weapon aimed in his direction.

Near another ridge, they crossed a creek that was little more than a spring seep. They followed the ridge awhile and then the trail widened and they moved back downhill and up again. Each rise and fall of the land looked like what had come before. The mountain air was thin and if Sinkler hadn't been hauling water such distances he wouldn't have had the spunk to keep going. They went on, the trees shading them from the sun, but even so he grew thirsty and kept hoping they'd come to a stream he could drink from. Finally, they came to another spring seep.

"I've got to have some water," he said.

Sinkler kneeled beside the creek. The water was so shallow that he had to lean over and steady himself with one hand, cupping the other to get a dozen leaky palmfuls in his mouth. He stood and brushed the damp sand off his hand and his knees. The woods were completely silent, no murmur of wind, not a bird singing.

"You want any?" he asked, but Lucy shook her head.

The trees shut out much of the sky, but he could tell that the sun was starting to slip behind the mountains. Fewer dapples of light were on the forest floor, more shadows. Soon the prisoners would be heading back, one man fewer. Come suppertime, the ginks would be spooning beans off a tin plate while Sinkler sat in a dining car eating steak with silverware. By then, the warden would have chewed out Vickery's skinny ass but good, maybe even fired him. The other guards, the ones he'd duped even more, would be explaining why they'd recommended making Sinkler a trusty in the first place.

When the trail narrowed again, a branch snagged Lucy's sleeve and ripped the frayed muslin. She surprised him with her profanity as she examined the torn cloth.

"I'd not think a sweet little gal like you to know words like that."

She glared at him and Sinkler raised his hands, palms out.

"Just teasing you a bit, darling. You should have brought another dress. I know I told you to pack light, but light didn't mean bring nothing."

"Maybe I ain't got another dress," Lucy said.

"But you will, and soon, and like I said it'll be a spiffy one."

"If I do," Lucy said, "I'll use this piece of shit for nothing but scrub rags."

She let go of the cloth. The branch had scratched her neck and she touched it with her finger, confirmed that it wasn't bleeding. Had the locket been around her neck, the chain might have snapped, but it was in her pocket. Or so he assumed. If she'd forgotten it in the haste of packing, now didn't seem the time to bring it up.

As they continued their descent, Sinkler thought again

about what would happen once they were safely free. He was starting to see a roughness about Lucy that her youth and country ways had masked. Perhaps he could take her with him beyond their first stop. He'd worked with a whore in Knoxville once, let her go in and distract a clerk while he took whatever they could fence. The whore hadn't been as young and innocent-seeming as Lucy. Even Lucy's plainness would be an advantage—harder to describe her to the law. Maybe tonight in the hotel room she'd show him more reason to let her tag along awhile.

The trail curved and then went uphill. Surely for the last time, he figured, and told himself he'd be damn glad to be back in a place where a man didn't have to be half goat to get somewhere. Sinkler searched through the branches and leaves for a brick smokestack, the glint of a train rail. They were both breathing harder now, and even Lucy looked tuckered.

Up ahead, another seep crossed the path and Sinkler paused.

"I'm going to sip me some more water."

"Ain't no need," Lucy said. "We're almost there."

He heard it then, the rasping plunge of metal into dirt. The rhododendron was too thick to see through. Whatever it was, it meant they were indeed near civilization.

"I guess we are," he said, but Lucy had already gone ahead.

As Sinkler hitched the sagging pants up yet again, he

decided that the first thing he'd do after buying the tickets was find a clothing store or gooseberry a clothesline. He didn't want to look like a damn hobo. Even in town, they might have to walk a ways for water, so Sinkler kneeled. Someone whistled near the ridge and the rasping stopped. As he pressed his palm into the sand, he saw that a handprint was already there beside it, his handprint. Sinkler studied it awhile, then slowly rocked back until his buttocks touched his shoe heels. He stared at the two star-shaped indentations, water slowly filling the new one.

No one would hear the shot, he knew. And, in a few weeks, when autumn came and the trees started to shed, the upturned earth would be completely obscured. Leaves rustled as someone approached. The footsteps paused, and Sinkler heard the soft click of a rifle's safety being released. The leaves rustled again but he was too worn out to run. They would want the clothes as well as the money, he told himself, and there was no reason to prolong any of it. His trembling fingers clasped the shirt's top button, pushed it through the slit in the chambray.

Nothing Gold Can Stay

Yes, I guess you could call them that, Mr. Ponder answered when Donnie asked if he'd brought back any war souvenirs. This was eight years ago. Mr. Ponder was already an old man then, his hearing almost gone along with half his teeth. He had a bad hip too, which was why he hired Donnie and me to paint and shingle his farmhouse, paying two fifteen-year-olds half what a grown man would work for. We'd ride our bikes from town and be there by eight. Quitting time was supposed to be five, but a few extra minutes always passed before he came out and told us to stop. Funny how that watch of his runs slow only at quitting time, I'd tell Donnie. That old man won't cut you much slack, Ben Reece at the hardware store had warned. But it paid more than cutting lawns.

Our only break was thirty minutes for lunch. We'd sit

on the porch and eat what he brought out, usually bologna sandwiches and chips, cans of Coke to wash it down with. He'd eat with us, but never said much except to complain about spilt paint or bent nails. Part of it was him being nearly deaf, but Ben had told us Mr. Ponder had never been outgoing, even before his wife had died. All that summer we were out there, no one but the mailman stopped by, and all he did was stick a few bills and advertisements in the rusty mailbox and drive on.

But this one day, Donnie said something about joining the Marines when he turned eighteen, and Mr. Ponder started telling us about fighting the Japanese in World War Two. On them islands you weren't even a man anymore, he told us. It's a wonder any of us could come back and be human again.

It was an unsettling thing to listen to, not just the stories about men burned alive and bodies blasted up into trees but how Mr. Ponder told it, not in the bragging way you might expect, or angry and hard-eyed. His voice was soft and he looked at us the whole time almost tenderly. When he finished, Donnie and me looked down at our half-eaten sandwiches, not sure what to do or say, waiting for Mr. Ponder to finish his sandwich or complain about something we hadn't done right, but he kept sitting there in the chair across from us. His eyes were damp. I looked over at Donnie and saw he was thinking the same thing as me—that if someone didn't say something, Mr. Ponder might start crying right in front of us. Donnie asked if he'd brought back anything from the war. Like souvenirs, I mean, Donnie stammered. That's when Mr. Ponder said he guessed you could call them that and Donnie asked if he'd like to show us. After a few moments, he said maybe we should see them and we went into the front room. A battered footlocker was between the TV and couch, and Mr. Ponder took some magazines off the top and opened it.

Donnie whispered that he bet it was a Japanese pistol or knife, that or a sword or flag. Mr. Ponder fumbled around in the locker a few more moments until he found what he wanted. He lifted a pint jar, and his gnarled hand held it out before us. It was one-third filled with what looked like gold buttons. Think about what a man has to become to do such a thing, he told us, and then that man be back home a year before it felt wrong. I've thought many a time to bury them, but I never can do it. It's like that would be getting off too easy somehow. He had placed the jar back in the paper bag. Anyway, Mr. Ponder had told Donnie and me, the next time you see one of them war movies that makes it all seem a lark, think about what's in this jar. Then he'd placed the jar back in the locker. The rest of the summer he never said another word about war or much else.

"The way I figure it," Donnie says, "that old man still owes us. Hell, he was paying us half what he should've. We worked harder for him than we ever did on that road oil crew."

Donnie gets up from the kitchen table and goes to the refrigerator. It and the TV are the last things left in the trailer that can be plugged into a socket. Microwave, VCR, air conditioner, they've all been pawned, or like his car, repoed. He still has electricity, but the front room's curtained windows and the one bare bulb make the room feel like a root cellar. Not that there's much to see other than empty cans and pizza boxes, in the corner a generator and a welding machine we haven't yet sold, that and a couple of four-cell aluminum flashlights stolen from the same construction site. Donnie comes back with two beers and hands me one.

"You been listening to me or not?" Donnie asks. "That Beck fellow in Asheville says he'll pay twelve hundred an ounce. Twelve hundred. There's got to be close to three ounces in that jar. We'll have to break into a shitload of them snowbirds' places to make that."

"Did you tell him what it is?"

"I told him and he said so what, that it all gets melted down anyway. He don't give a damn. Hell, he told me a medical student brings him a couple of gold crowns a month."

Donnie looks at me. He's still lit up but he won't be much longer and I won't either.

"What we got left?" I ask.

Donnie takes the plastic pill bottle from his front pocket and twists off the cap. He gives the bottle a shake and two tabs fall onto the table. I'm hoping hard they're pinks.

"Snake eyes," he says.

He leaves the two 10s on the table, rubs a fingertip over one like he wants to make sure it's real. He's thinking about swallowing it, though he knows he better wait.

"With that kind of money, Marvin will cut his price enough for us to deal some ourselves. I might even get my wheels back."

"Ponder hardly ever leaves that house," I say.

"We'll go at night when he's asleep," Donnie says. "He couldn't hear worth a shit eight years ago. You could run hounds through that house and he'd not know."

"But if he does, or sees the flashlight," I say. "He's got at least one gun in there, and you know he can kill a man."

"I'm willing to chance it," Donnie says. "I'll be the only one inside. Both of us go in there we'll just trip over each other. All you got to do is drive and help me get in a window. We do it tonight and this time tomorrow we'll be in high cotton."

I haven't had anything all day and the craving's working on me. My eyes are on the tabs and I can't get them to look elsewhere. I'm owed fifty dollars for a load of wood I cut, but the guy's been dodging me. I'll have to drive all over the county to track him down. I put the OC in my mouth and swallow what's left of the beer. Donnie takes his too. I think how there was a time a 10 would have me walking on sunshine half a day, but now it just takes the edge off.

"Ain't you tired of all this nickel-and-diming," Donnie says, "having to hustle up money every fucking day?"

"If we could just steal a few scrips," I say.

"You know that ain't happening," Donnie says. "Even Marvin can't get them anymore."

We sit there a few minutes. Donnie's right. I am tired of the nickel-and-diming. Sometimes it's a temp job on a construction crew or cutting firewood, sometimes shoplifting or breaking into a vacation home. It's always just enough. Come morning you're back where you were the day before. Just a week where it wasn't that way would be like taking a vacation, just floating along the way they do on those cruise ships, everything taken care of.

"Just steal the jar and leave, right?" I ask.

"I know you're the one that made the good grades at school," Donnie says, "but give this old boy some credit. I'm not fool enough to dawdle in there. It'll be like special ops. Identify the target, get in, and get my ass out quick."

"What time?"

"We leave here at midnight," Donnie says.

"We better wear dark clothes."

Donnie smiles.

"You mean like ninjas?"

"A black T-shirt and jeans."

"Sure," Donnie says.

I get up from the table.

"You can stick around here till then," Donnie says.

I shake my head and get out my keys. Even though I'm starting to feel the OC, the trailer's stifling. I live in an old mill house with a leaky roof and rotting boards, but at least it's not like being in a storage shed. Donnie follows me outside. It's one of those nice June evenings when the air cools off soon as the sun starts to fall, the day's heat making the coolness all the better.

"We used to haul in some nice trout right before dark," Donnie says.

"We did."

"That was something how we could work our asses off all day and still have the starch to wade that river two hours," Donnie says. "I guess when you're young like that you can do most anything."

"I reckon so," I say.

We stare out toward Balsam Mountain. I know we're both remembering how good those evenings were. We'd wade into the river wearing nothing but our jeans and tennis shoes. We'd throw some water on our hair and chests and let it clean off the heat and sweat and grime. Sometimes we'd catch trout and sometimes we wouldn't, but that didn't much matter.

Donnie smiles at me.

"Hell, we ain't even twenty-five yet and talking like we're ready for the rest home. When we cash in tomorrow, we'll buy some gear and hit the river, catch us a bunch of trout. Get a case of beer and fry those bad boys up."

I nod though I know it won't happen.

"Yeah, that's what we'll do," Donnie says. "It'll be same as it ever was. I bet there's even one of them big rainbows holding beneath Three-Mile Bridge, except this time I'll catch it instead of you."

I pick up Donnie at midnight and we drive out 107 and turn onto Mr. Ponder's dirt road. The few houses and trailers we pass have all their lights off, the folks inside enjoying the sleep of the righteous. We round a curve and the head-lights slash across a battered mailbox with "Ponder" on it. The house is dark. I drive another quarter mile and turn around, drive back slow.

"It'd likely be fine to just pull off on the side," Donnie says, but when I get to where the cornfield was I turn in.

I shut off the lights and bump across a few old rows, far enough to where someone going by won't notice the truck. I turn around to face the road and cut the engine. Donnie turns on his flashlight and I do the same. As we get out, he pulls something from the back of his jeans. His hand settles around the handle and I glimpse steel.

"Chill, buddy," he says. "It's just a screwdriver to prize a window or that locker."

There's a couple of big white oaks between the field and

Mr. Ponder's house, so we use them for extra cover. A big-bellied yellow moon is out, a few stars too. We palm the flashlights so just enough light leaks out to see a step ahead. His bedroom is at the back, so we step up on the porch, moving cautious so the boards don't creak. The front door is to the left of the window. Donnie nods at me to try the knob, just on the off chance. It turns.

"Damned if he ain't invited us in," Donnie whispers, placing his hand where mine was. "Go on back to the truck. If a light comes on, you be ready to haul ass."

He opens the door slow and goes in. I cup the beam and walk back to the truck and wait. The window's down but the cool air can't stop me from sweating. All the while I'm looking toward the house. A smudge of light shows for a moment in the front room. Then it's gone. I know it's Donnie's flashlight but I can't help thinking that if I saw it out here someone inside could have seen it too. The OC's worn off and I'm wishing bad I'd kept that last tab for now. I take my pack of cigarettes off the dash and light one. That helps a little, enough to finally let my mind drift a bit.

I think about those evenings on the river, not just the year we worked for Mr. Ponder but the summer after Donnie and me turned sixteen and worked on the highway department's road oil crew. That was hard work too, especially since the older guys gave us the shit jobs. But we still went to the river most evenings, even the summer after our junior year, at least until we began hanging out with some hard-living guys on the road oil crew.

The best time was always right before dusk. The water got quieter, more still, especially the deep pools. Sometimes there'd be a mayfly hatch, and it looked like pebbles hitting the surface. It was the trout feeding, but they wouldn't make splashes, just those tiny sips, as if even they didn't want to break the stillness. Donnie and me would break down our rods, knowing a spinner wouldn't work with a hatch going. But we wouldn't go right on home. We'd sit on the bank a few minutes. Donnie might smoke a cigarette but otherwise neither of us hardly moved. It was like the stillness had settled inside us too. The kinds of things that could fill a mind at such times—bad stuff at home, wondering if you'd cut it in the Marines or have money enough to go to A-B Tech—didn't seem so worrisome.

I'm so deep in the back-then that it takes a door slamming shut to remember where I am now. In front of Mr. Ponder's house, a flashlight's full beam slides across the ground a few moments before sweeping upward through tree branches and into the sky. Whoever it is, it's like he's sending up flares. The light jerks down and settles right on the truck and I'm wondering if whoever's holding that flashlight is also holding a gun. Then I hear singing and know it's Donnie. He comes toward me, jerking the flashlight this way and that as he sings a Jamie Johnson song.

"Damn, Donnie," I say when he gets in. "He might not hear but he can damn well see. He can still call the law."

"We've got no worries that way," Donnie says, but I'm watching for a light to come on as I crank the truck and drive out of the field.

I don't take an easy breath till we're past the farmhouse, and my arms are still shaking when Donnie turns on the overhead light. He's got a paper bag in his hand that looks to be the same one as eight years ago.

"We hit the jackpot tonight, son," he says, and takes out the mason jar and shakes it. "Like when we was kids and had piggybanks, but what's in here sure ain't copper. I got us more than this jar too."

"We said we'd not take anything else," I say.

"I wouldn't have," Donnie says, "but it was too quiet in there. I mean, an old man like that's going to snore or at least breathe heavy. I finally checked out the bedroom to see if he was even in the house. He was laid out on that bed and deader than a tarred stump. His clothes were on and arms at his sides like he was just waiting for the coffin."

"You're sure," I say, "I mean, about him being dead?"

"Dude, I'll spare you the details," Donnie says, "but he's been dead at least a couple of days."

Donnie reaches into the paper bag and takes out some bills.

"His billfold was on the bureau. Forty-six dollars that

he'll need no more than this," he says, reaches back into the bag and takes out a dental bridge, lays it on the dash beside the pack of cigarettes. "One that old has some prime gold in it."

Donnie stuffs the money in his jean pocket and wads up the paper bag and throws it on the floorboard. The jar is between his legs and he grips it with his left hand, uses his right to twist the metal ring. It doesn't give. He taps around the rim with the flashlight and tries again. I hear the rust grind as Donnie unscrews the ring. After he pries the lid off with the screwdriver, he takes the dental bridge off the dash and drops it in with the teeth, reseals the jar as best he can, and sets it between us.

"Damn," Donnie says, still breathing hard. "That old man works our asses off even when he's dead."

The dirt road ends and I turn right onto 19-23. We cross over the bridge and come into town, everything shut down except the Quik-Stop. We pass the bank, its sign lit up with the time and temperature.

"Hell, it ain't but one thirty and we got money," Donnie says. "I vote we go on over to Asheville. There's a place Jody Barnes told me about that don't shut down till daylight hits the windows. We'll find two girls who'll party with us, cash in come morning, and party some more."

I don't have a better idea so I say okay.

"Want to clean up first, put on some nice duds," Donnie

says, "or let the girls know from the start the rough outlaws that we are?"

"Let's go on," I say.

"OK," Donnie says, "but let's run by Marvin's first. It'll make for a better ride."

I don't answer, just turn right at the stoplight and drive toward Marvin's. I watch the headlights race ahead of us. Even going through town, we haven't met a single car or truck. Usually I'd figure that as some good luck, but tonight it feels more like a judgment.

"What's got you so quiet?" Donnie asks after a while.

"That dental bridge," I say. "You shouldn't have taken it."

"Why the hell not?" Donnie says. "We've stolen a thousand times more from live folks. If you're going to get all sorry about something, be sorry for them it matters to. It sure as hell don't matter to that old man."

Donnie slides a cigarette out of the pack and lights it, takes a couple of drags before he speaks again.

"Are we through talking about this?"

"Yeah," I say.

"Good."

In a couple of minutes we pull into Marvin's driveway. The front porch light comes on and I dim the lights and cut the engine.

"I'll be back in a minute," Donnie says and takes the jar with him.

He steps up on the porch and Marvin opens the door, nothing on but a pajama bottom. He doesn't look happy to be woke up, but he and Donnie talk a few moments and Marvin opens the door wider and steps back.

Donnie comes out a few minutes later with the jar in one hand and a pill bottle in the other.

"Son of a bitch was pissed at first, it being so late and all, but he sure changed his tune once I showed him the jar and he got his scales out. Three and three-quarter ounces. What does that come to by your ciphering?"

"Forty-five hundred."

"Exactly," Donnie says, "though Marvin had to tally it on paper. Anyway, we put four thousand of that in his pocket and he'll charge us twelve. We sell to some of those hotshot punks over at the high school at twenty and we'll glide a long while. It ain't like we got to decide right this instant, but I'm telling you, it all sounds like a sweetheart deal to me."

Donnie rattles the pill bottle.

"Hell, Marvin didn't even want the money for these. Just said not to worry, that we'd settle up later. Get us some beer to wash these down with and we'll be riding the magic carpet all the way to Asheville."

We head back through town and pull into the Quik-Stop. A bell tinkles when we enter and a man comes out of the stockroom. The place seems to change hands every other week, so it's not surprising I've never seen this guy.

No one else is in the store or parking lot and he looks nervous as Donnie opens the cooler, takes out a six-pack.

"This is enough, don't you think?" he says, and I nod.

We're heading for the counter when Donnie notices the rack of fishing equipment at the back of the store. There's a couple of dusty Zebco rods and reels leaning beside the rack. Donnie gives me the beer and picks one up to check the price, clicks the button to see if the line comes out smooth, and does the same to the other.

"We'll come back for these when we get paid," Donnie says.

"It's two o'clock," the man at the counter says. "I'm closing now."

Donnie turns, the rod in his free hand.

"Your sign says you're open all night."

"I'm closing now," the man says again.

He glances out at the parking lot and you can tell he's wishing hard someone would pull in, or even drive by. But nothing is moving out there. It's just him and me and Donnie under the store's bright lights.

"Take the beer," he says. "It's free."

"Well, that's neighborly of you," Donnie says, and sets the rod down, takes the beer from me.

"Is it Christmas or something?" Donnie says, a big grin widening on his face. "Everywhere we go people are giving us stuff."

"Go now," the man says.

As Donnie heads toward the door, I pull a five out of my wallet and step toward the counter. The man raises a hand as if to fend off a blow.

"Go now," he pleads.

"Okay," I say, stuff the bill in my pocket, and follow Donnie out to the truck.

I pull out of the parking lot. As soon as we're out of town, Donnie hands me a pink, takes one for himself. I put the tab on my tongue and let it lay there. Donnie opens a beer and hands it to me.

"Drink up," he says.

The OC's coating starts to dissolve. Its bitterness fills my mouth but I want the taste to linger a few more moments. As we cross back over the river, a small light glows on the far bank, a lantern or a campfire. Out beyond it, fish move in the current, alive in that other world.

Something Rich and Strange

S he follows the river's edge downstream, leaving behind her parents and younger brother who still eat their picnic lunch. It is Easter break and her father has taken time off from his job. They have followed the Appalachian Mountains south, stopping first in Gatlinburg, then the Smokies, and finally this river. She finds a place above a falls where the water looks shallow and slow. The river is a boundary between Georgia and South Carolina, and she wants to wade into the middle and place one foot in Georgia and one in South Carolina so she can tell her friends back in Nebraska she has been in two states at the same time.

She kicks off her sandals and enters, the water so much colder than she imagined, and quickly deeper, up to her kneecaps, the current surging under the smooth surface.

She shivers. On the far shore a granite cliff casts this section of river into shadow. She glances back to where her parents and brother sit on the blanket. It is warm there, the sun full upon them. She thinks about going back but is almost halfway now.

She takes a step and the water rises higher on her knees. Four more steps, she tells herself. Just four more and I'll turn back. She takes another step and the bottom is no longer there and she is being shoved downstream and she does not panic because she has passed the Red Cross courses. The water shallows and her face breaks the surface and she breathes deep. She tries to turn her body so she won't hit her head on a rock and for the first time she's afraid and she's suddenly back underwater and hears the rush of water against her ears. She tries to hold her breath but her knee smashes against a boulder and she gasps in pain and water pours into her mouth. Then for a few moments the water pools and slows. She rises coughing up water, gasping air, her feet dragging the bottom like an anchor trying to snag waterlogged wood or rock jut and as the current quickens again she sees her family running along the shore and she knows they are shouting her name though she cannot hear them and as the current turns her she hears the falls and knows there is nothing that will keep her from it as the current quickens and quickens and another rock smashes against her knee but she hardly feels it as she snatches another breath and she feels the river fall and she falls with it as water whitens around her and she falls deep into the whiteness and as she rises her head scrapes against a rock ceiling and the water holds her there and she tells herself don't breathe but the need rises inside her beginning in the upper stomach then up through her chest and throat and as that need reaches her mouth her mouth and nose open and the lungs explode in pain and then the pain is gone as bright colors shatter around her like glass shards, and she remembers her sixth-grade science class, the gurgle of the aquarium at the back of the room, the smell of chalk dust that morning the teacher held a prism out the window so it might fill with color, and she has a final, beautiful thought— that she is now inside that prism and knows something even the teacher does not know, that the prism's colors are voices, voices that swirl around her head like a crown, and at that moment her arms and legs she did not even know were flailing cease and she becomes part of the river.

The search and rescue squad and the sheriff arrived at the falls late that afternoon. Two of the squad members were brothers, one in his early twenties, the other thirty. They had a carpentry business, building patios and decks for lawyers and doctors from Greenville and Columbia who owned second homes in the mountains. The third man, the diver, was in his early forties and taught biology at the county high school. The sheriff looked at his watch and figured they had two hours at most before the gorge darkened. Even so the diver did not hurry to put on his wet suit and air tanks. He smoked a cigarette and between puffs talked to the sheriff about the high school's baseball team. They had worked together before and knew death punched no time clock.

When the diver was ready, a length of nylon rope was clasped tight under his arms. The older, stronger brother held the other end. The diver waded into the river, the rope trailing behind him like a leash. He dipped his mask in the water, put it on, and leaned forward. The three men onshore watched as the black fins propelled the diver into the hydraulic's ceaseless blizzard of whitewater. The men on the bank sat on rocks and waited. With his free hand, the older brother pointed upstream to a bend where he'd caught a five-pound trout last fall. The sheriff asked what he'd used for bait but didn't hear the answer because the mask bobbed up in the headwater's foam.

The brother tightened the slack and pulled but nothing gave until the others grabbed hold as well. They pulled the diver into the shallows and helped him onto shore. Between watery coughs he told them he'd found her in the undercut behind the hydraulic. She had been upright, her head and back and legs pressed against a rock slab. Only her hair moved, its long strands streaming upward. As the diver had drifted closer, he saw that her eyes were open. Their faces were inches apart when he slipped an arm around her waist. Then the hydraulic ripped free the mask and mouthpiece, grabbed the dive light, spiraling it toward the darkness.

The diver told the men kneeling beside him that the girl's blue eyes had life in them. He could feel her heart beating against his chest and hear her whispering. Before or after your mask was torn off, the sheriff asked. The diver did not know, but swore that he'd never enter the river again.

The younger brother scoffed, while the older spoke of narcosis though the pool was no more than twenty feet deep. But the sheriff did not dismiss what the diver said. He too had seen strange and inexplicable things involving the dead but had never mentioned them to others and did not choose to now. We'll find another way, he said, but that river has to lower some before I allow anyone else in there.

The diver had trouble sleeping afterward. Every night when he closed his eyes, he saw the girl's wide blue eyes, the flowing golden hair. His wife slept beside him, her body curled into his chest. They had no children and now he was glad for that. He had seen a picture of the parents in the local paper. They had been on the shore, within thirty feet of the undercut that held their daughter, the expressions on their faces beyond grief.

On the third night, the diver fell into a deeper sleep and the girl came with him. They were in the undercut again but now the river was tepid and he could breathe. As he embraced her, she whispered that this world was better than the one above and she should never have been afraid. He emerged in his wife's embrace. It's just a bad dream, she kept saying until he quit gasping. His wife closed her eyes and was quickly asleep, but he could not so went into the kitchen and graded lab tests until dawn.

The girl remained in the river. Volunteers cast grappling hooks from the banks and worked them like lures through the pool or stood in shallows or on rocks and jabbed with long metal poles. Some of the old-timers suggested dynamite but the girl's parents would not hear of it. The sheriff said what they needed was a week without rain.

The diver slept little the next few nights. In class he placed the students in small groups and had them discuss assigned chapters among themselves. He knew they talked about the prom instead of pupae and chrysalides, but he didn't care. On the third afternoon, he skipped the teacher's meeting and sat alone in his classroom. The school, emptied of students, was quiet, the only sound the gurgle of the aquarium. He would never speak to anyone, not even his wife, about what happened in the classroom's stillness, but that evening he told the sheriff he'd dive for the girl again.

Days passed. Rain came often, long rains that made every fold of ridge land a tributary and merged earth and water into a deep orange-yellow rush. Banks disappeared as the river reached out and dragged them under. But that was only surface. In the undercut all remained quiet and still, the girl's transformation unrushed, gentle. Crayfish and minnows unknitted flesh from bone, attentive to loosed threads.

Then the rains stopped and the river ran clear again. Boulders vanished for weeks reappeared. Sandbars and stick jams regathered in new configurations. The water warmed and caddis flies broke through the river's skin to make their brief flights before falling back into their element.

The sheriff called the diver and told him the river was low enough to try again. The next day they walked the half mile down the path to the falls. There were five of them this time, the sheriff, his deputy, the two brothers, and the diver. The sheriff insisted on two ropes, making sure they stayed taut. The water was clearer than last time and offered less resistance. The diver entered the abeyance as though parting a curtain, the river suddenly muted.

She was less of what she had been, the blue rubbed from her eyes, flesh freed from the chandelier of bone. He touched what once had been a hand. The river whispered to him that it would not be long now.

When he returned to shore, he told them her body was gone, not even a scrap of clothing or bone. He told them the last hard rain must have swept her downstream. The younger brother said the diver should go back and search the left and right sides of the falls. He argued the body could still be there. The deputy suggested they lower an underwater camera into the pool.

The sheriff shook his head and said to let her be. The men walked up the trail, back toward their vehicles, their lives. The midday sun leaned close and dazzling. Dogwoods bloomed small white stars. The diver knew in the coming days the petals would find their way into the river, drifting onto sandbars and gilding the backs of pools, and the diver knew some would drift through the rapids and over the falls into the hydraulic. They would furl amid the last bones and like the last bones they would finally slip free.

Cherokee

With a green rabbit's foot clipped on his belt loop, a silver four-leaf clover dangling from his neck, Danny has brought all the good luck he could find. As they drive past a billboard advertising Harrah's Casino, his free hand caresses the green fur, maybe hoping luck really can rub off on you. Lisa remembers a story about a magic lamp that, once rubbed, grants three wishes. Danny would settle for just one—make the one hundred and fifty-seven dollars in her handbag turn into a thousand.

"By what time Monday morning?"

"Ten," Danny answers.

"Does the bank come and get it or do we take it to them?"

Danny shifts his eyes from the road and looks at her.

"We could win," he says. "People do all the time. That

woman from Franklin won twenty thousand on a quarter slot machine."

Lisa watches the end of the odometer slip from nine to zero. 56240 miles. That's nine thousand more than when they'd bought the truck. Yet the Ranger looks every bit as clean as when they'd driven it off the lot eleven months ago. Every Sunday, Danny vacuums the interior with a Dustbuster, then washes the exterior. The tires glisten with Armor All. We really can't afford it, she'd told Danny that day at the Ford dealership, but she hadn't stopped the smooth-talking salesman from taking out his calculator and showing them that with the right financing they could. Lisa remembers how proud Danny had been when the last document was signed and the salesman handed him the key.

Even before Danny's hours got cut at the concrete plant, Lisa knew all it would take was a bit of bad luck—sickness or accident or layoff—to lose the truck. Lisa almost expected it, because she'd seen it happen to their neighbors at the apartment complex, to her friends, and to her own parents. She had kept those fears to herself though. Danny was a good husband. He'd been rowdy in high school, but once he and Lisa married he quit running with his buddies, quit smoking too. On Saturday nights when they went to The Firefly to dance and hear the band, Danny stopped at two beers. She's got you living straight, some of his buddies said when he turned down a drink. Unlike a lot of her girlfriends' husbands, Danny didn't spend money on expensive rifles or fishing rods, fancy boots or belts. He took a lunch to work.

Lisa drove the truck nearly as often as Danny did, and it was nice to finally have a vehicle whose radio and heater worked, that didn't risk stalling at every stop sign. In their three years of marriage, they'd both worked hard, Danny pouring concrete and Lisa clerking at the Bi-Lo, but had little to show for it. The apartment they rented had old cigarette burns on the carpet and cracks in the ceiling, windows with views of more brick walls. Except for Saturday nights, she and Danny rarely went out. It was good to have something to show for the hard work. Danny acted proud as a child with a new toy, but that boyishness was what had attracted Lisa to him in high school. Even when Danny got into trouble, it was for something like skipping class or setting a frog loose in the cafeteria. Boyish also in that he always believed that the next time, unlike the last, he'd somehow get away with it.

As they near Exit 81, more billboards appear on the roadside. On them, winners cup hands to gather spills of silver coins. Others spread bills in front of their faces like church fans and even the empty-handed laugh and smile. Danny releases the rabbit foot and clicks on the turn signal. He follows a line of cars onto the off-ramp and turns right like the others. More billboards appear, advertising everything from Santa Land to a gold and ruby mine.

"I should have listened to you," Danny says. "We wouldn't be in this mess if I had."

"We needed something that wouldn't break down every week," Lisa answers. "If I'd been late another time, I'd likely be out of a job."

"But it didn't need to be this new a truck. That was my wanting, not yours."

"I've enjoyed this truck as much as you have."

Lisa settles her hand on his upper arm, feels the bicep. Danny had been on the skinny side until he'd started spreading concrete, but now his arms, like his shoulders and chest, have thickened. When they dance on Saturday nights, those arms guide her so effortlessly that the weight of everything the week has laid on her, complaining customers, a crabby shift boss, is swept away.

"I've learned from this, I swear I have," Danny says, "even if we do win."

"Maybe we will," Lisa says, wanting also to believe it could happen. She touches the rabbit's foot. "It's not for lack of trying."

They pass the wooden sign that says Cherokee Indian Reservation and the traffic quickly becomes more stop than go. Tourists fill the sidewalks, most carrying shopping bags, some lapping ice-cream cones or sipping soft drinks. A child in a coonskin cap tugs at his mother's skirt. An old couple peer at a restaurant menu. *There is something for everyone*, one of the billboards claims, and Lisa sees that is so.

"Damn," Danny says. "It wasn't near this big when I came last time."

Ahead, the hotel and casino loom, blocking out even the mountains. It's the largest building Lisa has ever seen, and the brick exterior makes it appear impenetrable as a fortress. How could anyone hope to win against such a place, she wonders, yet as they enter the underground parking garage the first deck is completely full. They find a space on the second level and make their way across the shadowy deck to where bold red letters announce ENTRANCE TO CASINO like a final warning.

In the lobby a guard stands by the escalator. He checks their IDs and nods them past. The escalator descends into a loud brightness, the smell of cigarettes. Acres of gambling machines spread out left and right. Men and women of every sort sit before them on stools, coaxing colors and sounds from the machines as speakers pulse a backbeat of old rock songs. Danny nods toward a bar. He gets a beer but Lisa says she'll wait. Danny takes her hand and leads her into the nonsmoking section.

"We ain't got a player's card," Danny tells her, "so we have to use the slots."

"How many times did you come here?" Lisa asks.

"Twice," Danny says.

"And you lost both times?"

"Yeah," Danny says as he sits down between two other players, "but third time's the charm, right?"

There is hope but also enough doubt in his voice to make it a real question.

"We can bet one dollar or a hundred," he says. "You okay with ten?"

Lisa nods and takes the roll of bills from her pocketbook, gives him a ten.

"Watch how I do this," Danny says. "That way you can try too."

The machine sucks the ten-dollar bill out of sight. A bright-red cherry dominates the screen, beneath it the row of tumblers. Numbers that show winning combinations and their payoff are in the upper corner. The tumblers turn and resettle. Danny touches a button and only two tumblers spin the next time.

"Nothing," Danny mutters, and slides the next ten into the machine, then another, and another.

Because of the racket around her, Lisa can't concentrate enough to understand how the game is played, what should be saved or not saved, what combinations other than three in a row win. When she hands Danny the next ten, he asks if she'd like to try.

"No," she says. "I wouldn't know what I was doing."

"Like I do," Danny snorts, and turns back to the machine.

Lisa takes two more tens from the roll to have them ready, then looks around. A gray-bearded man is seated to their left, using only his right hand because his other shirtsleeve is empty. *Vietnam Vet* is printed on his camo ball cap. Opposite him is a guy wearing a black Metallica T-shirt. A long leather wallet protrudes from his pocket, its chain attached to a belt loop. He looks no older than Lisa. She waits for Danny to free another bill from her hand. When he doesn't, Lisa looks back at the machine.

The credit line has a 40 on it.

"So we're ahead?" she asks.

As quickly as Danny nods, the 40 becomes a 30 and she can't help but think just saying they were ahead had jinxed the spin.

Danny pushes the button again. Two cherries appear and he saves them. The middle tumblers spin and a third cherry drops in between the other two. The machine whoops and chimes as 530 appears on the credit line.

"You spun them right that time, son," the one-armed vet says.

The Metallica fan looks at Danny's screen as well but says nothing.

"Halfway there," Danny says, and the slots roll again.

The young guy loses and curses. He glares at the machine, then reaches for his billfold. Lisa glances at the vet's credit line. It's only two dollars but he seems more amused than angry when it slips to one. He wears a gold watch and Lisa is surprised to see over an hour has passed. There are no clocks in the casino, Lisa suddenly notices, windows either. A person could be down here and not know if it was morning or afternoon or night or even what day it was.

Danny's credit line goes down to 420 but after a half hour it's back up to 640. He stands and places his hands on his hips, stretches backward.

"I'm going to get another beer."

"I can fetch it for you," Lisa offers.

"No, I need to move around a bit," Danny says. "Just stay on the stool until I get back."

Lisa does what he says, watching the machine.

"They used to call these things one-armed bandits," the vet says, smiling at Lisa as he speaks. "You reckon that's the why of me not winning?"

Lisa, unsure how to answer, just smiles back. The vet swivels on the stool to face her.

"Where you all from?"

"Sylva," Lisa says.

"I'm from over that way too," the vet says. "Glenville."

"That's not far from us," Lisa says, her eyes still on the credit line.

"Up to 640," he says. "You about to cash out?"

"Not yet," Lisa answers.

"You'd be crazy to," the Metallica fan says, entering the conversation. "You get these damn machines in a mood to give it up you best stay on them."

Danny comes back and Lisa gets up. When Danny settles on the stool, the vet holds out his hand.

"Lucas Perkins, but I go by Perk. I hear we're near about neighbors."

"He's from Glenville," Lisa says.

"Danny Hampton," Danny says as they shake. "Good to meet you."

"Good to meet you too," Perk says, and pauses. "Can I ask a favor?"

"What sort of favor?" Danny asks.

"Let me put ten in on your next try."

"I don't think that's a good idea," Danny says.

"Just one time," Perk says, and offers Danny the bill. "I just want a touch of luck, just so I can remember what it feels like."

"What if I lose?" Danny asks.

"Then you ain't done nothing but what I'd do my own self."

Danny hands the ten to Lisa, changes the bet to 20 and presses the button. The numbers settle and he saves a cherry. The tumblers spin and a 7 and another cherry appear.

"There you go," Perk says.

"Give him twenty," Danny says.

As Lisa peels off two tens, the Metallica fan mutters something and turns back to his machine. Perk tucks the bills in his pants pocket, gestures at the beer can as he gets up.

"Let me buy you and your lady here a drink."

"No thanks," Danny says. "I'd as soon not risk a DUI."

"I figured you two to be staying in the hotel."

"No," Danny answers.

"How about a drink for you," Perk asks Lisa.

Lisa thinks how at least a Coke or bottled water would be nice, but she shakes her head.

"Mind if I rub that rabbit's foot?" Perk asks. "I'm going to try poker with what I got left. Maybe I'll have enough luck to at least lose slow."

"Sure," Danny says.

He rubs the green rabbit's foot between his index finger and thumb.

"Maybe one day I can do you all a good turn too," Perk says, and disappears into the maze of machines.

When the credit line hits 700, Danny pauses to take a long drink from the beer can. The casino is warm and cigarette smoke drifts into the nonsmoking section. Lisa's thirsty but she's not about to leave Danny's side until they've won or lost. Perk's stool remains unoccupied. The younger guy watches Danny's credit line instead of playing his machine.

For the next hour, the line rises and falls. It reminds Lisa of a kite in a gusting wind, rising but never quite able to hold on to the sky. When the credit line falls to 480, the Metallica fan catches Lisa's eye, smiles smugly. So that's what you're waiting around for, Lisa thinks. His smile vanishes as the numbers rise again.

Perk returns, a plastic room key in his hand.

"Still ahead, I see."

Danny nods.

"I come out three hundred ahead," he says, and offers Lisa the key. "It's paid for, in cash, so the minibar is on your dime."

"You ought not have done that," Danny says. "You don't owe us anything."

"Figure it a bit more luck then," Perk says, still holding the key out to Lisa. "If you don't use it, it'll just go to waste, including the free breakfast."

Lisa takes the key, thinks how if she and Danny lose the 157 dollars they came with, they can figure the money went to a night in a swanky hotel.

"Thank you," Lisa says.

"Glad to do it," Perk says. "If you're ever over in Glenville, look me up."

Lisa watches him ascend on the escalator. At the top, Perk glances back and doffs the bill of his cap, though to her and Danny or all the players she cannot tell. Lisa checks the credit line and it's at 480, 470, 460. Two wild cherries appear on the screen and Danny saves them, pushes the button, and a third drops into the middle slot as if fallen from a tree. The machine makes its noises and 960 appears on the credit line.

"We made it," Danny says.

His voice is like a still pond, soft and calm, as if afraid he might startle the machine and cause the numbers to re-arrange.

"It's not a thousand," Lisa says.

"It is with the money in your handbag," Danny answers.

"You're not thinking about cashing in," the young guy says. "You got to ride this kind of luck out."

"I don't *got* to do anything," Danny says.

He's staring at the 960, and Lisa knows there are other numbers spinning in Danny's head, two thousand, three thousand, five. He's thinking about a year's rent paid up, enough money set aside to start a family, that the jerk next to them may be right. Lisa knows he's thinking these things because she is too. She waits for him to look up at her and say it aloud.

Instead, Danny punches the cash-out button and a white slip emerges.

"Boy, you need to grow a pair," the Metallica fan says, turns and walks away.

For a moment, Danny looks ready to go after the guy, but then his face settles into a smile. They find an exchange machine and Danny puts the white slip in and nine one-hundred-dollar bills slide out, each so new looking you could believe the machine made them on the spot, three twenties equally crisp.

"Want to head back home?" Danny asks, his tone suggesting he would.

"No, let's stay," Lisa says. "It'd be a shame to waste a free hotel room and breakfast. They hardly charge for food and drink, so we can celebrate and still leave with the thousand. It'll be like a minivacation."

"All right," he says. "I'm hungry, so let's get something to eat."

They go to a restaurant and eat their fill of fried chicken and vegetables, a thick wedge of pecan pie topped with ice cream. Afterward, Lisa wants to go straight to the bar, but Danny says they need to make sure they can get in the room. They ride the elevator up to the sixth floor and follow the numbers down the hallway. It's the most beautiful hotel room Lisa has ever been in, nicer even than the one in Gatlinburg where she and Danny spent their honeymoon. A crystal chandelier hangs from the ceiling and a thick maroon carpet muffles their steps. On one side of the room is a small bar with a glass mirror, and opposite, a canopied bed whose pillowcases and bedspread look as if they've never been wrinkled. Lisa goes to the window, touches the plush velvet drapes as she looks out at mountains turning bluer and bluer as they stretch westward into Tennessee. Danny comes over to look as well.

"It's such a pretty view," Lisa says. "I bet some of those mountains go far as Knoxville."

"Probably so," Danny says.

Lisa presses her palm against Danny's cheek and lifts her mouth to his. She thinks about taking him by the hand

and leading him to the bed, but there will be time enough for that later tonight and in the morning too.

"Let's go," she says. "I'm going to get me one of those fancy-colored drinks with an umbrella in it."

They sit at the bar and Lisa chooses a piña colada from the plastic drink menu. Danny orders a draft beer, same as he'd get at The Firefly. When the drinks arrive, they turn their seats and watch the players at their machines. The lights and noise remind Lisa of the county fairs of her childhood. Only a Ferris wheel is missing. When she finishes her drink, Danny's glass is half full, but he tells Lisa to go ahead and order herself another. Her next drink is so blue it shimmers within the glass. Soon the casino's bright lights begin to blur. The vibrating bass connects her whole body to the music. Lisa wishes she and Danny could dance, but there's no dance floor.

Her glass is empty, Danny's as well. Two drinks are usually her limit, but it feels so good to be away from everything familiar, to have the kind of luck, twice, that people hardly ever get. She can't help thinking it's the best day of her and Danny's life together, better than the night they got engaged or their first Christmas, even their wedding day.

"Third time's the charm, right," Lisa says as she looks over the drink list.

"It was today," Danny says.

Lisa gets the bartender's attention and orders her drink

and, though he doesn't ask her to, another beer for Danny. This drink is green and sweeter than the others, like liquid candy. She sips and watches the players. Many rise from their stools empty-handed, but a few carry white slips over to the exchange machines. A woman in a blue jumpsuit is hugging a man at a poker machine as an employee hands them a stack of bills.

"Why don't they have a white slip?" Lisa asks.

"If you win over a thousand," Danny says, "an employee has to pay you."

Lisa scoots her chair closer to the bar, her eyes on Danny as well as the machines. He watches the players intently, but with yearning or just curiosity she cannot tell. Two thousand, three thousand, four thousand, five. In the alcohol haze it's as though the numbers are rolling out in front of her. Shouldn't two pieces of good luck lead to a third, she tells herself. The straw sucks air and Lisa peeks beneath the little umbrella, confirms the glass is empty. The room tilts and Lisa almost loses her balance when she sets her glass on the bar. She giggles. Danny opens her handbag, takes out a twenty and a ten, and lays them on the bar.

"You're my lucky boy," Lisa says as he guides her through the casino, up the escalator, and across the walkway to the hotel.

Danny doesn't remove his arm until they are in the room. When he does, the pastel walls shift. Lisa flops onto the bed and grins up at him.

"Come keep this girl company," she says, but the room is tilting more now. She shuts her eyes so it can settle.

When Lisa opens her eyes, her throat is parched and her head aches. It is light outside, enough to make her want to pull the drapes. The bedside clock says 9:20. She turns over and finds Danny's side is vacant. He's not in the bathroom or on the balcony.

She stays in bed a few minutes longer, then gets up and dresses. She doesn't look in her handbag, doesn't want to look. Instead, she goes down the hall to the elevator. Lisa watches the numbers light up and then go dark as she descends. The elevator door opens and she steps into the lobby. The breakfast section is bustling. Elderly women wearing purple hats and name tags crowd around a waffle maker, children scamper around the room. A man who looks as hungover as Lisa grimaces at the poached egg on his paper plate.

As Lisa is about to head for the walkway, she sees Danny seated alone in their midst, a Styrofoam coffee cup in his hand. Something shifts inside her with an almost audible click. When she opens the handbag, all the money is there. The elevator closes behind her, and she walks toward a man who knows as well as she does that their luck couldn't last.

Where the Map Ends

They had been on the run for six days, traveling mainly at night, all the while listening for
the baying of hounds. The man, if asked his
age, would have said forty-eight, forty-nine, or fifty—he
wasn't sure. His hair was close-cropped, like gray wool
stitched above a face dark as mahogany. A lantern swayed
by his side, the twine securing it chafing the bullwhip
scar ridging his left shoulder. With his right hand he
clutched a tote sack. His companion was seventeen and
of a lighter complexion, the color of an oft-used gold coin.
The youth's hair was longer, the curls tinged red. He carried the map.

As foothills became mountains, the journey became
more arduous. What food they'd brought had been eaten
days earlier. They filled the tote with corn and okra from

fields, eggs from a henhouse, apples from orchards. The land steepened more and their lungs never seemed to fill. I heard that white folks up here don't have much, the youth huffed, but you'd think they'd at least have air. The map showed one more village, Blowing Rock, then a ways farther a stream and soon a plank bridge. An arrow pointed over the bridge. Beyond that, nothing but blank paper, as though no word or mark could convey what the fugitives sought but had never known.

They had crossed the bridge near dusk. At the first cabin they came to, a hound bayed as they approached. They went on. The youth wondered aloud how they were supposed to know which place, which family, to trust. The fugitives passed a two-story farmhouse, prosperous looking. The older man said walk on. As the day waned, a cabin and a barn appeared, light glowing from a front window. Their lantern remained unlit, though now neither of them could see where he stepped. They passed a small orchard and soon after the man tugged his companion's arm and led him off the road and into a pasture.

"Where we going, Viticus?" the youth asked.

"To roost in that barn till morning," the man answered. "No folks want strangers calling in the dark."

They entered the barn, let their hands find the ladder, and then climbed into the loft. Through a space between boards the fugitives could see the cabin window's glow.

"I'm hungry," the youth complained. "Gimme that lantern and I'll get us some apples."

"No," his companion said. "You think a man going to help them that stole from him."

"Ain't gonna miss a few apples."

The man ignored him. They settled their bodies into the straw and slept.

A cowbell woke them, the animal ambling into the barn, a man in frayed overalls following with a gallon pail. A scraggly gray beard covered much of his face, some streaks of brown in his lank hair. He was thin and tall, and his neck and back bowed forward as if from years of ducking. As the farmer set his stool beside the cow's flank, a gray cat appeared and positioned itself close by. Milk spurts hissed against the tin. The fugitives peered through the board gaps. The youth's stomach growled audibly. I ain't trying to, he whispered in response to his companion's nudge. When the bucket was filled, the farmer aimed a teat at the cat. The creature's tongue lapped without pause as the milk splashed on its face. As the farmer lifted the pail and stood, the youth shifted to better see. Bits of straw slipped through a board gap and drifted down. The farmer did not look up but his shoulders tensed and his free hand clenched the pail tighter. He quickly left the barn.

"You done it now," the man said.

"He gonna have to see us sometime," the youth replied.

"But now it'll be with a gun aimed our direction," Viticus hissed. "Get your sorry self down that ladder."

They climbed down and saw what they'd missed earlier.

"Don't like the look of that none," the youth said, nodding at the rope dangling from a loft beam.

"Then get out front of this barn," his companion said. "I want that white man looking at empty hands."

Once outside, they could see the farm clearly. Crop rows were weed choked, the orchard unpruned, the cabin itself shabby and small, two rooms at most. They watched the farmer go inside.

"How you know he got a gun when he hardly got a roof over his head?" the youth asked. "The Colonel wouldn't put hogs in such as that."

"He got a gun," the man replied, and set the lantern on the ground with the burlap tote.

A crow cawed as it passed overhead, then settled in the cornfield.

"Don't seem mindful of his crop," the youth said.

"No, he don't," the man said, more to himself than his companion.

The youth went to the barn corner and peeked toward the cabin. The farmer came out of the cabin, a flintlock in his right hand.

"He do have a gun and it's already cocked," the youth said. "Hellfire, Viticus, we gotta light out of here."

"Light out where?" his companion answered. "We past where that map can take us."

"Shouldn't never have hightailed off," the youth fretted. "I known better but done it. We go back, I won't be tending that stable no more. No suh, the Colonel will send me out with the rest of you field hands."

"This white man's done nothing yet," the man said softly. "Just keep your hands out so he see the pink."

But the youth turned and ran into the cornfield. Shaking tassels marked his progress. He didn't stop until he was in the field's center. The older fugitive grimaced and stepped farther away from the barn mouth.

The farmer entered the pasture, the flintlock crooked in his arm. Any indication of his humor lay hidden beneath the beard. The older fugitive did not raise his hands, but he turned his palms outward.

The white man approached from the west. The sunrise made his eyes squint.

"I ain't stole nothing, mister," the black man said when the farmer stopped a few yards in front of him.

"That's kindly of you," the farmer replied.

The dawn's slanted brightness made the white man raise a hand to his brow.

"Move back into that barn so I can feature you better."

The black man glanced at the rope.

"Pay that rope no mind," the farmer said. "It ain't me put it up. That was my wife's doing."

The fugitive kept stepping back until both of them stood inside the barn. The cat reappeared, sat on its haunches watching the two men.

"Where might you hail from?" the farmer asked.

The black man's face assumed a guarded blankness.

"I ain't sending you back yonder if that's your fearing," the farmer said. "I've never had any truck with them that would. That's why you're up here, ain't it, knowing that we don't?"

The black man nodded.

"So where you run off from?"

"Down in Wake County, Colonel Barkley's home place."

"Got himself a big house with fancy rugs and whatnot, I reckon," the farmer said, "and plenty more like you to keep it clean and pretty for him."

"Yes, suh."

The farmer appeared satisfied. He did not uncock the hammer but the barrel now pointed at the ground.

"You know the way over the line to Tennessee?"

"No, suh."

"It ain't a far way but you'll need a map, especially if you lief to stay clear of outliers," the white man said. "You get here last night?"

"Yes, suh."

"Did you help yourself to some of them apples?"

The black man shook his head.

"You got food in your tote there?"

"No, suh."

"You must be hungry then," the farmer said. "Get what apples you want. There's a spring over there too what if your throat's dry. I'll go to the cabin and fix you a map." The white man paused. "Fetch some corn to take if you like, and tell that othern he don't have to hide in there lest he just favors it."

The farmer walked back toward the cabin.

"Come out, boy," Viticus said.

The tassels swayed and the youth reappeared.

"You hear what he say?"

"I heard it," the youth answered and began walking toward the orchard.

They ate two apples each before going to the spring.

"Never tasted water that cold and it full summer," the youth said when he'd drunk his fill. "The Colonel say it snows here anytime and when it do you won't see no road nor nothing. Marster Helm's houseboy run off last summer, the Colonel say they found him froze stiff as a poker."

"You believing that then you're a chucklehead," Viticus said.

"I just telling it," the youth answered.

"Uh-huh," his elder said, but his eyes were not on the youth but something in the far pasture.

Two mounds lay side by side, marked with a single creek stone. Upturned earth sprouted a few weeds, but only a few. The youth turned from the spring and looked as well.

"Lord God," he said. "This place don't long allow a body to rest easy."

"Come on," Viticus said.

The fugitives stepped back through the orchard and waited in front of the barn. The farmer was on his way back, a bucket in one hand and the flintlock in the other.

"Why come him to still haul that gun?" the youth asked.

The older man's lips hardly moved as he spoke.

"Cause he ain't fool enough to trust two strangers, specially after you cut and run."

The farmer's eyes were on the youth as he crossed the pasture. He set the bucket before them and studied the youth's face a few more moments, then turned to the older fugitive.

"There's pone and sorghum in there," the farmer said, and nodded at the bucket. "My daughter brung it yesterday. She's nary the cook her momma was, but it'll stash your belly."

"Thank you, suh," the youth said.

"I brung it for him, not you," the farmer said.

The older fugitive did not move.

"Go ahead," the farmer said to him. "Just fetch that pone out the bucket and strap that sorghum on it."

"Thank you, suh," the older fugitive said, but he still did not reach for the pail.

"What?" the white man asked.

"If I be of a mind to share . . ."

The white man grimaced.

"He don't deserve none but it's your stomach to miss it, not mine."

The older fugitive took out a piece of the pone and the cistern of sorghum. He swathed the bread in syrup and offered it to the youth, who took it without a word. Neither sat in the grass to eat but remained standing. When they'd finished, the older fugitive set the cistern carefully in the bucket. He stepped back and thanked the farmer again but the farmer seemed not to hear. His blue eyes were on the youth.

"You belonged to this Colonel Barkley feller too?"

"Yes, suh," the youth said.

"Been on his place all your life."

"Yes, suh."

"And your momma, she been at the Colonel's awhile before you was born."

"Yes, suh."

The farmer nodded and let his gaze drift toward the barn a moment before resettling on the youth. "The Colonel got red hair, has he?"

"You know the Colonel?" the youth asked.

"Naw, just his sort," the farmer answered. "You call him Colonel. Is he off to the war?"

"Yes, suh."

"And he is a Colonel, I mean rank?"

"Yes, suh," the youth answered. "The Colonel got him up a whole regiment to take north with him."

"A whole regiment, you say."

"Yes, suh."

The white man spat and wiped a shirtsleeve across his mouth.

"I done my damnedest to keep my boy from it," he said. "There's places up here conscripters would nary have found him, but he set out over to Tennessee anyway. You know the last thing I told him?"

The fugitives waited.

"I told him if he got in the thick of it, look for them what hid behind the lines with fancy uniforms and plumes in their hats. Them's the ones to shoot, I said, cause it's them sons of bitches started this thing. That boy could drop a squirrel at fifty yards. I hope he kilt a couple of them."

The older fugitive hesitated, then spoke.

"He fight for Mr. Lincoln, do he?"

"Not no more," the farmer said.

To the west, the land rose blue and jagged. The older fugitive let his eyes settle on the mountains before turning back to the farmer. The youth settled a boot toe into the grass, scuffed a small indentation. They waited as they had always waited for a white man, be it overseer, owner, now this farmer, to finish his say and dismiss them.

"The Colonel," the farmer asked, "he up in Virginia now?"

"Yes, suh," the older fugitive said, "least as I know."

"Up near Richmond," the youth added. "That's what the Miss's cook heard."

The farmer nodded.

"Black niggers to do his work and now white niggers to do his fighting," he said.

The sun was full overhead now. Sweat beads glistened on the white man's brow but he did not raise a hand to wipe them away. The youth cleared his throat while staring at the scuff mark he'd made on the ground. The farmer looked only at the older fugitive now.

"I need you to understand something and there's nary a way to understand it without the telling," the farmer said to the other man. "Them days after we got the word, I'd wake of the night and Dorcie wouldn't be next to me. I'd find her sitting on the porch, just staring at the dark. Then one night I woke up and she wasn't on the porch. I found her here in this barn."

The farmer paused, as if to allow some comment, but none came.

"Me and Dorcie got three daughters alive and healthy and their young ones is too. You'd figure that would've been enough for her. You'd think it harder on a father to lose his onliest son, knowing there'd be never a one to carry on the family name after you ain't around no more. But he was the youngest, and womenfolk near always make a fuss over a come-late baby."

"That rope there in the barn," the farmer said, lifting a Barlow knife from his overall pocket. "I've left it dangling all these months 'cause I pondered it for my ownself, but every time I made ready to use it something stopped me."

The farmer nodded at a ball of twine by the stable door and tossed the knife to the older fugitive.

"Cut off a piece of that twine nigh long as your arm."

The fugitive freed the blade from the elk-bone casing. He stepped into the barn's deep shadow and cut the twine. The farmer motioned with the flintlock.

"Tie his hands behind his back."

The other man hesitated.

"If you want to get to Tennessee," the farmer said, "you got to do what I tell you."

"I don't like none of this," the youth muttered, but he did not resist as his companion wrapped the rope twice around his wrists and secured it with a knot.

"Toss me my Barlow," the farmer said.

The older fugitive did, and the farmer slipped the knife into his front pocket.

"All right then," the farmer said, and nodded at the tote. "You got fire?"

"Got flint," the other man said.

The farmer nodded and removed a thin piece of paper from his pocket.

"Bible paper. It's all I had."

The older fugitive took the proffered paper and unfolded it.

"That X is us here," the farmer said, and pointed at a mountain to the west. "Head cross this ridge and toward that mountain. You hit a trail just before it and head right. There comes a creek soon and you go up it till it peters out. Climb a bit more and you'll see a valley. You made it then."

"And him?" the man said of the youth.

"Ain't your concern."

"It kindly is," the man said.

"Go on now and you'll be in Tennessee come nightfall."

The youth's shoulders were shaking. He looked at his companion and then at the white man.

"You got no cause to tie me up," the youth said. "I ain't gonna be no trouble. You tell him, Viticus."

"He'd not be much bother to take with me," the older fugitive said. "I promised his momma I'd look after him."

"You make the same promise to his father?" the farmer said and let his eyes settle on the older fugitive's shoulder. "From the looks of that scar, I'd notion you to be glad I'm doing it. I'd think every time you looked at that red hair of his you'd want to kill him yourself."

"I didn't mean to hide from you," the youth said, his breathing short and fast now. "I just seen that gun and got rabbity."

"Go on now," the farmer told the older fugitive.

Two hours later he came to the creek. The burlap tote hung over one shoulder and the lantern hung from the other. He began the climb. The angled ground was slick and he grabbed rhododendron branches to keep from tumbling back down.

There was no shingle or handbill proclaiming he'd entered Tennessee, but when he crested the mountain and the valley lay before him, he saw a wooden building below, next to it a pole waving the flag of Lincoln. He stood there in the late-afternoon light, absorbing the valley's expansiveness after days in the mountains. The land rippled out and appeared to reach all the way to where the sun and earth merged. He shifted the twine so it didn't rub the ridge of scar. Something furrowed his brow a few moments. Then he moved on and did not look back.

PART
II

A Servant of History

A servant of history. Since accepting his employ with the English Folk Dance and Ballad Society, that was how Wilson thought of himself and, in truth, a rather daring servant. He was no university don mumbling Gradgrindian facts facts facts in a lecture hall's chalky air, but a man venturing among the new world's Calibans. On the ship that brought him from London, Wilson explained to fellow passengers how ballads lost to time in Britain might yet survive in America's Appalachian Mountains. Several young ladies were suitably impressed and expressed concern for his safety. One male passenger, an uncouth Georgian, had acted more amused than impressed, noting that Wilson's "duds" befit a dancing master more than an adventurer.

After departing the train station and securing his belongings at the Blue Ridge Inn, Wilson walked Sylva's main thoroughfare. The promise of the village's bucolic name was not immediately evident. Cabins and tepees, cattle drives and saloons, were notably absent. Instead, actual houses, most prosperous looking, lined the village's periphery. On the square itself, a marble statue commemorated the Great War. Shingles advertised a dentist, a doctor, and a lawyer, even a confectioner. The men he passed wore no holsters filled with "shooting irons," the women no boots and breeches. Automobiles outnumbered horses. It had all been immensely disappointing. Until now.

The old man was hitching his horse and wagon to a post as Wilson approached. He did not wear buckskin, but his long gray beard and tattered overalls, hobnailed boots, and straw hat bespoke a true rustic. The old man spurted a stream of tobacco juice as an initial greeting, then spoke in a brogue so thick Wilson asked twice for the words to be repeated. Wilson haltingly conveyed his employer's purpose.

"England," the rustic said. "It's war you hell from?"

"Pardon?" Wilson asked, and the old man repeated himself.

"Ah," Wilson said. "Where do I hail from?"

The rustic nodded.

"Indeed, sir, I do come from England. As I say, I am in search of British ballads. Many of the old songs that have vanished in my country may yet be found here. But as a visitor to your region, I have little inkling who might possess them. The innkeeper suggested an older resident, such as yourself, might aid me."

Wilson paused, searching the hirsute face for a sign of interest, or even comprehension. He had been warned at the interview that the expedition would be challenging, especially for a young gentleman fresh out of university, one, though this was only implied, whose transcript reflected few scholarly aspirations. In truth, Wilson had been the Society's third choice, employed only when the first decided to make his fortune in India and the second staggered out of a pub and into the path of a trolley.

"Of course, aside from my gratitude, I have leave to pay a fair wage for assistance in locating such ballads."

The old man spat again.

"How much?"

"Three dollars a day."

"I'll scratch you up some tunes for that," the rustic answered, and nodded at the wagon, "but not cheer. We'll have to hove it a ways."

"And when might we set out?" Wilson asked.

"Come noon tomorrow. You baddin at the inn?"

"Badding?"

"Yes, baddin," the old man said, "sleepin."

"I am."

"I'll pick you up thar then," the rustic said, and resumed hitching his horse.

"May I ask your name, sir," Wilson said. "Mine is James Wilson."

"I a go ba rafe," the old man answered.

They left Sylva at twelve the next day, Wilson's valise settled in the wagon bed, he himself on the buckboard beside Iago Barafe. They passed handsome farms with fine houses, but as they ventured farther into the mountains, the dwellings became smaller, sometimes aslant and often unpainted. To Wilson's delight, he saw his first cabin, then several more. They turned off the "pike," as Barafe called it, and onto a wayfare of trampled weeds and dirt. As the elevation rose, the October air cooled. The mountains leaned closer and granite outcrops broke through stands of trees. The remoteness evoked an older era, and Wilson supposed that it was as much the landscape as the inhabitants that allowed Albion's music to survive here.

He thought again of his university dons, each monotoned lecture like a Lethean submerging from which he retained just enough to earn his degree. Now, however, he, James Wilson, would show them that history was more than their ossified blather. It was outside libraries and lecture halls and alive in the world, passed down one tongue to another by the humble folk. Why even his guide, obviously illiterate, had a name retained from Elizabethan drama.

A red-and-black serpent slithered across the path, disappeared into a rocky crevice.

"Poisonous, I assume," Wilson said.

"Naw," Barafe answered, "nothin but a meek snake."

Soon after, they splashed across a brook.

"We're on McDawnell land now," the older man said.

"McDowell?" Wilson asked.

"I reckon you kin say it that way," Barafe answered.

"The family is from Scotland, I presume," Wilson said, "but long ago."

"They been up here many a yar," the old man said, "and it's a passel of them. The ones we're going to see, they got their great-granny yet alive. She's nigh a century old but got a mind sharp as a new-hone axe. She'll know yer tunes and anything else you want. But they can be a techy lot, if they taken a dislikin to you."

"If my being from England makes them uncomfortable," Wilson proclaimed, "that is easily rectified. My father is indeed English and I have lived in England all my life, but my mother was born in Scotland."

Barafe nodded and shook the reins.

"It ain't far to the glen now," he said.

The wagon crested a last hill and Wilson saw not a dilapidated cabin but a white farmhouse with glass windows and a roof shiny as fresh-minted sterling. Yet within the seemingly modern dwelling, he reminded himself, a near centenarian awaited. A fallow field lay to the left of the house, and a barn on the right. Deeper in the glen, cattle and horses wandered an open pasture, their sides branded with an *M*.

A man who looked to be in his fifties came out on the porch and watched them approach. He wore overalls and a chambray shirt but no sidearm.

"That's Luther," Barafe said.

"I presumed we might be greeted with a show of weaponry."

"They'd not do that less you given them particular cause," Barafe answered. "They keep the old ways and we're their guests."

When they were in the yard, Barafe secured the brake and they climbed off the buckboard and ascended the steps. The two rustics greeted each other familiarly, though their host addressed his elder as "Rafe." Wilson stepped forward.

"James Wilson," he said, extending his hand.

"Good to meet you, James," the other replied. "Call me Luther."

Their host took Wilson's valise and opened the door, then stood back so the guests might enter first and warm themselves in front of the corbelled hearth. The parlor slowly revealed itself. A carriage clock was on the mantel, beside it a row of books that included the expected family Bible but also a thick tome entitled *Clans of Scotland*. More of the room emerged. A framed daguerreotype of a white-bearded patriarch dominated one wall, on the opposite, a red-and-black tartan, its bottom edge singed. Two ladder-back chairs were on one side of the hearth and on the other a large Windsor chair plushly lined in red velvet.

"Please sit down," their host said. "I saw you coming from a ways off so stoked the fire for you."

A middle-aged woman entered the parlor with a silver platter. On it were bread and jelly and coffee, silverware and saucers, two cloth napkins. Luther placed a footstool between his guests, and the woman set the platter down.

"This is Molly," their host said, "my wife."

The woman blushed slightly.

"We just finished our noon dinner," she said. "If we'd known you were coming, we'd have waited."

Like Barafe, Luther and his wife had prominent accents, yet both spoke with a formality that acknowledged "d's" and "g's" on word endings. Barafe sat down and tucked his napkin under his chin with an almost comic flair. Wilson sat as well, only then saw that the Windsor chair was occupied.

The beldame's face possessed the color and creases of a walnut hull. A black shawl draped over her shoulders, obscuring a body shrunken to a child's stature. The old woman appeared more engulfed than seated, head and body pressed into the soft padding, shoe tips not touching the floor. And yet, the effect was not so much of a small woman as of a large chair, which, like the velvet lining, gave an appearance of regal authority.

"Granny," Molly said. "We have guests."

Wilson stood.

"I am pleased to make your acquaintance, madam," he said, and gave a slight bow.

"This here is James Wilson," Barafe said, suddenly impelled to use surnames. "He come all the way from England to learn old tunes."

The matriarch blinked twice and then stared fixedly at Wilson. Her eyes were of the lightest blue, as if time had rinsed away most of the color, but there was a liveliness inside them. Wilson sat back down.

"He's gonna learn 'em and haul 'em back to England," Barafe added, all but waving a Union Jack over Wilson's head.

"I do indeed come from England, madam," Wilson said, "but my mother is a proud Scot and I too proudly claim the heritage of thistle and bagpipe."

The proclamation was a bit disingenuous. Wilson's mother, though born in Scotland, had moved to London at sixteen and rarely spoken of her Scots roots. Nor had she encouraged her son to think of himself as anything but English. The sole acknowledgment was a blue-and-black tartan that hung, rather forlornly, on an attic wall. The old woman made no reply, and Wilson, wondering if he should summon forth other lore worthy of a loyal scion of Scotland, decided on a more direct tack.

"And of course I will gladly pay you for your trouble," Wilson added.

"If Granny learns you some songs, you'll pay no money for them," Luther said, "but it's her notion to do or not do."

At first it appeared that the matriarch might not deign to respond. Then the sunken mouth slowly unsealed, revealing a single nubbed tooth.

"I can sing a one," the old woman said, "but I'll need a sup of water first."

Wilson opened his valise and took out the fountain pen and ink bottle, a calfskin ledger. He set the ink bottle by his chair, opened the ledger, and wrote *Jackson County, United States, October 1922.*

"If you could give me the title of the ballad first, that would be helpful," Wilson said with proper deference.

"It's called 'The Betrothed Knight,'" the old woman answered.

Her voice was low but surprisingly melodic. Wilson wrote rapidly as the matriarch sang of a deceived maiden. Several words were pleasingly archaic, but even better for his purposes, the mention of a knight supported England as the ballad's place of origin. Dipping the pen into the ink during the refrain, Wilson set down all the words in one listening.

"That's a bully one," Barafe said.

"Yes," Wilson agreed. "Most excellent indeed. Do you know more, madam?"

The old woman appeared reluctant, so Wilson tried another approach.

"Your name will appear on the page with the ballad," he noted, "so you will be properly honored."

The appeal to vanity had the opposite effect intended. The old woman asked why she should get "notioned" for something that wasn't hers. She pulled the shawl tight around her neck and chin as if to muffle any further word or song. Luther went to the hearth and picked up the poker, stabbed at the fire until the slumbering flame sparked back to life. As their host leaned the poker by the hearth, Wilson saw that, by accident or design, the poker's prod was shaped like an *M*. Wilson nodded toward the bookshelf and its tome.

"Of course sharing your ballads does Scotland a great service as well," Wilson noted. "You are preserving a vital part of your ancestors' and descendants' history."

The old woman did not speak but her eyes were now attentive.

"And part of mine as well," Wilson reminded her, and racked his brain for something beyond the Merry Olde England perspective of Scotland as a mere barnacle on England's ship of empire.

Macbeth and a joke about bagpipes and testicles emerged first, then, wedged between William the Bruce and Bonnie Prince Charlie, a muddle of dates-feuds-clans and, finally, tam-o-shanters and tartans. *Tartans*. Wilson left the chair and walked over to the red-and-black tartan, let a thumb and finger rub the cloth. He nodded favorably, hoping to impart a Scotsman's familiarity with weave and wool.

"Our tartan hangs on a wall as well, blue and black it is, the proud tartan of Clan Campbell, and no doubt ancient as yours, though better preserved, which is to be expected, since ours has not traveled such distances."

"And not burned," the old woman said grimly.

Luther and Molly glared at Wilson, and despite the fire, a gust of cold air seemed to fill the room.

"Your tartan," Luther asked, "an azure blue?"

"Well, yes," Wilson answered.

"*Argyle*," the beldame hissed.

Wilson removed his finger and thumb from the tartan.

"Pardon me," he said. "I'm certain the tartan has been as well cared for as possible. It has just endured a longer journey than ours, across an ocean. And my touching it, I meant no disrespect."

Barafe looked up from his plate, finally aware that some drama was unfolding around him.

"What did you say to vex Granny *McDonald*?" Barafe asked.

For a few moments the only sound was the ticking of the clock. A disquieting thought nudged Wilson, some connection between English Kings and Argyle Campbells and, thanks to Iago Barafe's sudden gift of enunciation, Clan McDonald.

"Perhaps we should go," Wilson said, stepping over to

pack up his valise. "I'm sure we have taken up enough of your time."

"Not till I sing one more song," Granny McDonald said.

Luther latched the front door before crossing the room to the fireplace. He lifted the poker but, instead of poking the fire, nested the prod in the flames.

"You go on out and get your horse some water from the spring, Rafe," Luther McDonald said.

Wilson watched as Barafe hesitated, then gave his erstwhile charge a shrug and stood. Molly unlatched the door, locking it back after the old man passed through.

"This song," the old woman said, "it's called 'The Snows of Glencoe.' Be it one you know?"

"I do not, madam," Wilson stammered.

Wilson did, however, know about the Glencoe massacre. He had been roused from his usual classroom stupor when his don mentioned Clan *Campbell*'s involvement. That had sparked enough interest in Wilson to ask his mother about the event. It's all in the past, his mother had told him, and refused to say more.

"The previous ballad really will suffice," Wilson said. "I have another appointment and must be going."

"Sit down and listen," Luther McDonald said.

Wilson did as he was told and the beldame began to sing.

They came in a blizzard and we offered them heat
A roof o'er their heads and dry shoes for their feet

We wined them and dined them they ate of our meat
And slept in the house of McDonald.

Some died in their beds in the grasp of their foe
Some fled in the night and were lost in the snow
Some lived to accuse them who struck the first blow
That slaughtered the house of McDonald.

They came from Fort Henry with murder in mind.
The Campbells had orders Prince William had signed
Put all to the swords these words were underlined
And leave none alive named McDonald.

The old woman's lips tightened into a mirthless smile. For a few moments no one moved. Then Luther retrieved the poker from the fire, placed his free hand close enough to gauge the heat. Wilson withdrew a wallet from his back pocket.

"I wish to make payment for the songs as well as your hospitality," he said, and rapidly began pulling out bills.

"We'll take no money," his host answered. "No man, not even a king, can buy off a McDonald."

When his ship docked in London harbor six weeks later, Wilson's tongue had not fully healed. Months passed before he was able to convey his thoughts aloud, and during those mute months he showed little desire to do so with pen and paper. Nevertheless, the previously unknown ballad Wilson brought back caused a sensation, in part because its purveyor had placed himself in such peril to acquire it. One London newspaper proclaimed James Wilson worthy of mention with Sir Walter Raleigh and Captain John Smith, those earlier adventurers who also left their civilized isle to venture among the new world's Calibans.

Twenty-Six Days

It's almost twelve thirty when I'm done sweeping the front steps, so I go inside to stash the broom and dustpan and lock the closet. In the foyer, there's a crisis hotline flyer and a sign-up sheet beneath. Professor Wardlaw has volunteered for Friday, her usual night. I walk out of Cromer Hall and into a November day warmer and sunnier than you usually get in these mountains. The clock tower bell rings. In my mind I move the heavy metal hands ahead ten and a half hours. Kerrie is already in bed.

Over at the ATM, students pull out bank cards like winning lottery tickets. Probably not one of them ever thinks that while they're sitting in a classroom or watching a basketball game kids their own age are getting blown up by IEDs. I think again about how we wouldn't be in Afghanistan if there was still a draft. You can bet it'd be a lot different if everyone's kids could end up over there. *Just a bunch of stupid hillbillies fighting a stupid war*, that's what some jerk on TV said, like Kerrie and the rest don't matter. There's times I want to grab a student by the collar and say you don't know how good you got it, or I tell myself I've given my daughter more than my parents gave me. That's easier than thinking how if I'd had more ambition years back and gotten a welding certificate or degree at Blue Ridge Tech, made more money, Kerrie wouldn't be over there.

I cross the street separating the campus from town and go into Crawford's Diner. Professor Wardlaw's in a booth with Professor Maher and Professor Lucas, who also have offices in Cromer Hall. Ellen brings my plate quick as I sit down at the counter. She has it ready, since I get just thirty minutes for lunch. I eat free, a perk, like Dr. Blanton letting us use his computer. Ellen pours my ice tea and gives me a fork and knife and napkin.

"Not a good morning?" I ask, because Ellen's waitress smile looks frayed.

"It's been okay," she answers, speaking softer as she nods at the professors. "That one with the black hair is who said it, ain't she?"

"Yeah," I say, "but she didn't mean nothing by it, not really."

"When they came in, I had a notion not to serve them at all," Ellen says.

"You know she does a lot of good," I say.

"That still don't excuse her saying such a thing though," Ellen answers, and takes the water and tea pitchers off the counter.

I watch in the mirror as Ellen fills glasses and makes small talk, except at Professor Wardlaw's booth. Ellen lifts her eyes as she passes so that even if they do want something she'll not notice. I shouldn't have told her what Professor Wardlaw said, or made it worse by pointing her out in the parking lot. Ellen's as good a wife as a man could ask for, but she'll hold a grudge.

I check the wall clock. It's 12:50 so I finish and take the plate to the kitchen. Ellen's there changing an order and we talk a minute about Kerrie's application. I come back and the professors are going out the door, backpacks hanging from their shoulders. A single one-dollar bill is on the table. I follow them back to Cromer Hall. Someone's spilled a drink near the entrance, ice cubes scattered like dice across the floor. There's a folding yellow caution sign by the entrance, so I set it up. I'm walking down the hallway to get my mop and bucket when I hear my name. Professor Korovich is standing by her office door, a stack of books in her hands.

"I have these for Kerrie," she says.

I thank her and put them on the closet shelf beside the

paper towels and disinfectants. I lift the mop bucket to the sink and fill it, pour in the Lysol and head down the hall. Professor Wardlaw's office door is open but she's alone. I think about last month when Professor Korovich gave me some books for Kerrie. When I came back up the hall, Professor Wardlaw was in her office talking to Professor Maher. *Nadia doesn't realize that he'll just turn around and sell them, but better the flea market than the outhouse.*

I mop the foyer and put the caution sign back up. I get my broom and dustpan and sweep the stairwells, then empty the bathroom trash cans and clean the toilets and sinks. When the 3:30 bell rings, the last classrooms empty so I sweep them. Since tomorrow's a holiday, most of the faculty's gone home. I get out my master key and empty their trash cans. When I get to Professor Korovich's office, the light's still on. She's been at the college only since August and all her family is in Ukraine. Sometimes we talk about how hard it can be when you're separated from your loved ones.

I knock and she tells me to come in.

"How is Kerrie?" she asks, saying the name so the first part's longer than the last.

"She's doing fine," I tell her.

"Less than a month now?"

I nod as I empty her garbage can.

"Not so long," Professor Korovich says, and smiles.

I ask about her family. She tells me her mother's home

from the hospital and I tell her I'm glad to hear that. I thank her again for the books and close the door. By the time I've done all the offices, the hall clock says 4:20. I check the bathrooms a last time and punch out.

There's a note tucked under my windshield wiper from Ellen saying she's working till five. I think about going over to the café and having a cup of coffee but decide to wait in the truck. Sometimes I'll find a magazine in a trash can to bring home, but I don't have anything like that so I look over the books Professor Korovich gave me. Three are about teaching but one is called *Selected Stories of Anton Chekhov*. I open it and start reading a story about a man whose child has died. He tries to tell other folks what's happened but no one wants to hear it so he finally tells his horse. You'd think a story like that would be hokey, and maybe it is to some people, but when Ellen gets in the truck she asks if I'm okay. She says I look like I've been crying.

Before I can answer, Ellen raises her hands to her mouth.

"Kerrie's fine," I say quickly. "It's allergies or something."

Ellen's hands settle back in her lap but now they're woven together like she's saying a prayer. Maybe she is saying one.

"Kerrie's fine," I say again.

"You'd figure it would be soothing that she's made it this long," Ellen says as I pull out of the lot, "but the closer we get to her coming home, the scareder I am."

I put my hand on her shoulder and tell her everything's going to be fine. When we pass in front of the quad, we both check the clock.

"A bunch of folks came in for early supper and Alex asked me to stay," Ellen says.

"We'll be on time," I say.

"I did make an extra nine dollars just on the tips."

"That's good," I say, and smile. "You must have given them better service than I saw some folks get at lunch."

I stop at a crosswalk and a group of college students pass in front of us.

"Alex said something to me about that," Ellen says.

"They complain?"

"No, but Alex don't miss much."

Ellen nods at the books between us.

"Professor Korovich gave us some more?"

"Yes," I say. "Remind me to tell Kerrie."

We get lucky on the lights, three greens and one red, but once we pass the city limits sign a car is piddling along and I'm stuck behind it. The road's curvy and the driver's going thirty in a fifty-five zone. It's two miles before the road straightens and I can pass. By the time we pull into the lot that says PATIENT PARKING, we're running late but Dr. Blanton's car is still outside. We hurry in and I tell him we're sorry to be late.

"Don't worry about that," he says. "I'm just glad you won't miss your call."

He nods at the waiting room floor. There's a red stain wide as a tractor tire.

"A logger nearly cut his arm off this morning. Tonya and I got a lot of it up but the floor needs a good scouring."

"Yes sir," I say, and check the clock.

"I left five more dollars, for the extra work on the floor," Dr. Blanton says, and takes out his keys. "Tell Kerrie the man that brought her into this world says to be careful, doctor's orders."

"We'll tell her," Ellen says.

Dr. Blanton leaves and Ellen goes in to make sure the Skype camera works and that the chat is set up. I go to the storeroom and fill up the mop bucket, then add the bleach and set it in the lobby. It's time for Kerrie to call so I go into Dr. Blanton's office. Ellen's in the chair and I stand behind her. When the box comes up, Ellen clicks "answer." Kerrie appears on the screen and it's like every other time, because a part of Ellen and me that's been knotted up inside all day can finally let go.

Since it's already Thanksgiving over there, Ellen asks if they'll have turkey and dressing for lunch and Kerrie says yes but it won't taste nearly as good as what Ellen makes. When I ask how things are going, Kerrie says fine, like she always does, and tells us she has two more days before she has to go back out. Ellen asks about a boy in her unit who got hurt by an IED and Kerrie says he lost his leg but the doctors saved the sight in one eye.

For a few moments, nobody says anything, because we all know it could have been Kerrie in that Humvee one day earlier. Ellen asks about school. And Kerrie says the head of the education department at N.C. State is matching up the tuition costs with the army's college fund. They've been really helpful, she says. I tell her about the books and Kerrie says to be sure and thank Professor Korovich.

Maybe it's because the picture's a little blurry, but one second I see something in Kerrie's face that reminds me of when she was a baby, then something else reminds me of her in first grade and after that high school. It's like the slightest flicker or shift makes one show more than the others. But that's not it, I realize. All those different faces are inside me, not on the screen, and I can't help thinking that if I remember every one, enough of Kerrie's alive inside me to keep safe the part that isn't.

We stay on awhile longer, not saying anything important, but what we talk about doesn't matter as much as seeing Kerrie and hearing her voice, knowing that she's made it safe through one more day and night. Afterward, we clean up the office, mopping the waiting room last. The bloodstain's a chore. We get on our hands and knees, rubbing the linoleum so hard it's like we're trying to take it off too.

We finally get done and Ellen picks up the two twenties and the five on the receptionist's desk. The money we get from Dr. Blanton goes into an envelope we're giving Kerrie the day she gets home. It'll be nearly two thousand dollars, enough to help her some at college. On the way home I turn on the radio. It's a station Ellen and me like because it plays lots of songs we heard while dating, songs we listened to when we were no older than Kerrie.

Several stores already have their Christmas decorations up, and they brighten the town as we drive through. As I wait for a light to turn, I think about Ellen being more scared the closer we get to Kerrie coming home. It's like Kerrie's been lucky so long that the luck's due to run out. I can't help thinking that we can still get a phone call saying Kerrie's been hurt. Or even worse, a soldier showing up with his cap in his hands.

The light turns green and I pass the clock tower, behind it Cromer Hall. The office windows are all dark, but there are lights on at the student center. Some students won't be going home for the holidays, and because of that someone in town has a phone close by, ready if it rings. I think about a young woman who's hurt and scared making that call, and how someone will be there to listen.

A Sort of Miracle

Baroque wished he and Marlboro were back at the house watching medical shows with their sister, Susie. Instead, they were in a truck with Denton, their brother-in-law. Baroque wasn't used to Denton being this close. Denton was an accountant, and Monday through Friday he was at work all day. When he came home, he usually disappeared into the back bedroom after dinner. Of course Saturdays and Sundays Denton was around more, and often in the front of the house, and it was starting to take just a little thing like opening the refrigerator door for their brother-in-law to give Baroque and Marlboro a look, a real unfriendly look. One night Denton had called him and Marlboro lard-asses and claimed they lacked ambition and would never amount to anything if that didn't change. He'd said it just the one time, but Baroque could tell Denton had thought it more than one time. He and Marlboro had even sat on the porch for a few minutes yesterday, just to get somewhere Denton wasn't.

But they were with him now and they sure couldn't get away from him in a truck cab, and the three of them were riding up a bumpy dirt road in the Great Smoky Mountains National Park, doing something that Baroque was pretty sure wasn't just a little illegal, like smoking pot or running a stop sign, but a lot illegal, like getting sent to prison, regardless of Denton saying it was a public service. When Baroque asked why they had to go bear hunting this particular day, Denton said this cold spell would soon send the bears into hibernation. Marlboro had asked what hibernation was and Denton had answered that it was when dumb, lazy creatures laid around for months doing nothing.

The dirt road came to a dead end. Cinder blocks marked the parking lot, and there was a trail on the other side. Denton told them again everything they were supposed to do and handed Baroque the cell phone, then left with the pistol and knife strapped around his waist. Once up the trail a few yards, Denton was suddenly gone, like the woods had just swallowed him up. It made Baroque feel spooky, but everything about this bear business had been spooky. Like the way two weeks ago Denton had brought a big carton home after work and pulled out a steel trap, a pistol, a yellow box of bullets, and then a knife. A big knife, the kind

Baroque had seen only in movies where maniacs hacked people to death, maniacs who always had some mask or hood covering everything except their eyes, which made it worse, because it could be anybody who was the maniac, even the person in the movie who seemed most normal.

Like Marlboro, Baroque wore only a regular shirt and a sweatshirt. The warmth from the heater seemed to have whooshed right out the moment Denton opened the truck door. Baroque and Marlboro hadn't been with Denton when he set the bear trap, but Baroque wished now that Denton had made them come then instead of now, because it had to have been a lot warmer that day. His breath clouded the windshield and Baroque felt his body start to shiver. He looked at the trail, then cranked the engine and put the heater on high.

"Denton said we shouldn't do that unless we got real cold," Marlboro said.

"Well, I am real cold," Baroque said, "aren't you?"

Marlboro nodded and clapped his hands together and rubbed them.

"How cold do you think it is?"

"Eighteen degrees," Baroque said. "That was the number on the bank sign."

"I don't think we've ever been in weather like this," Marlboro said.

"No," Baroque agreed. "It's probably never been this cold in Florida, except maybe during the Ice Age."

"I wish Susie could have come down to Florida to help us get a job there instead of up here."

"That would have been better," Baroque said, "but there's nothing we can do about that."

"I guess this is our first job," Marlboro said, "being here, I mean."

"Yes, I guess it is."

"You think we'll lose our nose and fingers, like that guy on the medical show?"

"No," Baroque said. "That guy was stuck on a mountain-top three days. We won't be here that long."

"I sure hope not," Marlboro replied. "I don't think I could eat if I couldn't breathe through my nose."

"You'd learn to get used to it," Baroque said.

They listened to the heater hiss against the cold.

"You think he's really going to kill a bear?"

"That's what he said," Baroque answered.

As the cab warmed, the breath fogging the windshield evaporated, but all Baroque could see were woods, woods where someone or something could be watching him and Marlboro right now.

"It's sort of spooky when there aren't any streets or houses around," Marlboro said, evidently feeling the same way.

"It wouldn't hurt to lock our doors," Baroque said, "just to be on the safe side."

They pressed down the locks and for a few minutes didn't speak. It was Marlboro who broke the silence.

"He wouldn't just leave us out here, would he? I mean, he's not acted very friendly lately."

"No," Baroque said. "He'd have made us get out of the truck and driven off if he was going to do that."

Denton felt better as soon as he left the truck. Being that close to his brothers-in-law made him feel like a fungus was starting to grow on him. They both had a moldy sort of smell, like mushrooms. Which was no surprise, since Baroque and Marlboro moved about as much as mushrooms. They never left the house, and got up from the couch only to eat or go to the bathroom. Hell, mushrooms probably did more than that. They actually *grew*. They were finding nutrients, some kind of work was going on down there in the soil.

Baroque and Marlboro had been with him and Susie two months, up from Florida to find jobs, they claimed. Evidently they expected the jobs to haul themselves up to Denton's front porch and wait for Marlboro and Baroque to step out the door and be whisked away. Denton blamed a lot of it on their being from Florida. He'd never met anyone from the place who didn't get on his nerves, like all the Florida retirees who drove ten miles an hour on any road that wasn't straight and wide as an airport runway. Admittedly, Denton hadn't been around many younger Floridians, but his brothers-in-law were indictment enough. Baroque, whose name sounded a lot like *a roach* to Denton, was the older of the two by eleven months. Their father was a self-proclaimed "free spirit" who'd drifted like a spore— that's the way Denton always envisioned it, anyway—into Colorado and attached himself long enough to find Susie's mother and have a baby with her. Then the three of them drifted on down to Florida, where Baroque and Marlboro were born. It was the father who'd named the two boys. Susie didn't know how the name Baroque had come about, but Marlboro had been named after the Marlboro Man, the cigarette cowboy. Susie said it was meant as a comment on society. Thank God that Susie, at thirty the oldest by six years, had been named by the mother. Susie wasn't a Floridian, in Denton's view. She'd been born in Colorado and had gotten out of Florida quick as she could, earning a scholarship to Gulf Coast College, in Alabama. She met her first husband there, a fifty-year-old admissions coun- selor. As soon as Susie graduated, they married and moved to North Carolina, so mountains could blot out some sun. The first husband had problems with psoriasis. But he had at least gotten her to North Carolina, where she and Den- ton met.

Susie's first marriage hadn't worked out any better than Denton's. Her first husband had made Susie wear his dead aunt's Sunday church hat every time they had sex. An aw- ful thing, but Denton's first wife had been even worse. The admissions counselor's aunt might've been dead but at least the man hadn't lain there like *he* was dead. Denton's first wife was so frigid that each time they had sex she might as well have been embalmed. Eventually, every time they did it he'd hear organ music inside his head, the same kind that oozed out of funeral home walls. It was a wonder he and Susie could ever touch another naked person after the two partners they'd had.

The two of them had overcome a lot, no doubt about that, but now they had a nice marriage and a fine house and Denton had a good job as an accountant and Susie was the head nurse at the county clinic. Which was why she'd let Baroque and Marlboro come up from Florida in the first place. She'd wanted to help her brothers improve themselves, and Denton couldn't blame her for that. After all, hard as it was to believe, they were her brothers. She was even trying to get them, or at least Baroque, interested in medicine. Baroque was *sort of smart*, Susie claimed, and if Baroque got a job as a med tech maybe Marlboro could be an orderly or something. She'd taken them to the clinic with her for a day, and now she had them watching the medical shows. It might inspire them, she claimed, though Denton was of a mind that a good kick in their lardy asses would inspire them more.

Susie watched the medical shows as much as she could. She might need to know this sometime, she always said when Denton complained. He understood it could be helpful to someone in the medical field, but Susie didn't watch the shows about a heart transplant or a knee operation or a woman having a baby. Susie watched shows with names like *Medical Mysteries* or *I Survived*, shows about hundred-pound tumors or people who'd lost all their toes to frostbite or who internally combusted, and it all gave Denton the willies. He would go in the back room and watch the fourteen-inch TV on the bureau, catch the news on CNN and then maybe one of the business shows, or get on the computer, where he'd been doing the bear research. Anything was better than the medical shows. The worst thing to Denton was how they always ended. There'd be upbeat music and the announcer would talk about miracles, and the person who'd had the hundred-pound tumor or the man whose leg had been snapped off by a shark always acted like it was a *good thing* this had happened. Now Susie had Baroque and Marlboro watching them every night, probably even a few about bear attacks.

They did at least watch them. Whenever Denton ventured into the front room, their eyes were always on the screen. They weren't talking and seemed to be paying attention. Of course Baroque and Marlboro never did talk a lot anyway, not to Denton, or even much to Susie. They just sat next to each other, in the exact same posture, like twins. Part of that was surely their being less than a year apart in age, and also because Baroque and Marlboro did look like twins, at least in the face and especially their eyes, which changed when they shifted them in a different direction— less green to more brown or vice versa. It reminded Denton of his twelfth-grade biology project. The teacher had given every student in the class a jar of fruit flies, and after a while the fruit flies' eyes were supposed to change, and everybody else's fruit flies had changed eye color except Denton's. His just crawled around on the glass for an hour and then died. He got a D- on a major nine-week project, which was totally unfair. Denton hadn't picked out the flies or put them in the jar. He hadn't *asked* for them. They were just there on his desk one morning. He got no college-scholarship offers like Susie, and instead had to work his way through. The damn fruit flies had made sure of that.

Susie saw Baroque and Marlboro's interest in the medical shows as a step forward. Still, neither of them had actually left the house to apply for a med tech program or orderly job, and though Susie hadn't actually said it, Denton suspected even she was tired of her brothers being around. It had pretty much shut down their sex life, because their house was a fine house but a small one. Baroque was in the spare room with just three inches of drywall between him and their bedroom. Marlboro was on the couch, and if Denton and Susie could hear the springs squeak whenever Baroque or Marlboro turned over, then they sure as hell could hear what he and Susie were up to. After the nightmare sex of their first marriages, there had been issues to work out, which they had. Until the brothers-in-law showed up, Susie tended to moan some and rock the bed a good bit, but there wasn't much of that anymore, and now Denton was starting to have some *problems*, and Denton had never had *problems*, at least with Susie.

He stopped to rest a moment, checked to make sure the double-ply plastic bag was still in his coat pocket. Paws and gallbladder—that was all he needed. Denton had to hand it to the Chinese. They were smart, and had been smart a long time. They'd invented gunpowder and a lot of other things, even spaghetti. The Chinese also knew how to cure certain male *problems* without having to explain them to a doctor and then after that having to take the prescription to a pharmacy where some eighteen-year-old cashier would stop chewing her bubble gum just long enough to do something stupid like say your name and the name of what you were picking up out loud, maybe even say it over a speaker like it was a frigging pep rally. No, the Chinese understood better how to do things than Americans. They explained what cured a problem and explained where to get the cure and even how to prepare it. It was the right way of doing things, which was why they pretty much owned the United States now. The way he'd been feeling the last few months, Denton wasn't sure he'd mind the Chinese taking over America completely, because everybody over there worked. If they didn't they starved. Sure, times were hard here. Denton understood that as well as anyone. He'd barely survived a layoff himself. But unlike his brothers-in-law, he'd have found something to do if he'd been laid off, even if it was picking up cans and bottles out of ditches.

Denton moved on up the trail, wondering if a caught bear would stay quiet or make a ruckus. The only sound was the water, and not even that except where a waterfall or rapid was, all the stream's slow parts covered with ice. No other sounds like a chain saw or car or dog, because this was real wilderness he was in now, and it was so cold the birds and squirrels were using their energy just to hunker down and survive. Denton felt cold even with his thermal underwear, gloves, and wool coat, and it would only get colder, because though it was midafternoon, the sun would soon start to fade behind the mountains. At least the cold would be good for preserving the bear paws and gallbladder. Denton wouldn't even have to stop and get ice for the cooler, which meant five minutes less time before he could get some distance between him and his brothers-in-law.

Denton looked down through the trees to see if he could glimpse the truck but didn't see it. All Baroque and Marlboro had to do was sit and wait, that and lean on the horn if a ranger appeared. Even they would have trouble screwing up those directions. Then again, Denton wouldn't put it past them to drive over to Bryson City for something to eat or a six-pack of beer, then forget where the hell they'd been parked. That was the worst of it. Most people were smart at something. There were guys Denton had known in high school who weren't able to spell *cat*, but at least they could change their spark plugs or replace a blown fuse. Baroque and Marlboro didn't even possess smarts like that. Having clogged up the commode three times, Marlboro, it was clear, couldn't even figure out how to properly wipe his ass, and Baroque had driven the truck like a drunk ten-year-old the one time Denton allowed him to take it to town. Denton thought about calling them, just to be sure they hadn't driven off, but then he remembered they would actually need *money* to buy a hot dog or six-pack. Still, Denton was beginning to feel uneasy about bringing them along.

He went on, breathing hard because he was climbing steep ground, and having to be more careful too, since ice was on the trail this far up. That was something else. He'd figured, wrongly, that the cold weather would drive Baroque and Marlboro back to Florida. *Florida.* Denton said the word out loud. What kind of name for a state was that? It wasn't a word with any backbone to it, like the hard C in the first syllable of *Carolina.* You could look at Florida on a map and see that it drooped down from the rest of America like a limp peter. It was a wonder the founding fathers hadn't just sawed the damn state off and let it drift away. A state where the most famous *person* went around pretending to be an eight-foot-tall mouse. Every kid in the state had probably been to see that thing, walked up to it, and shaken its hand or paw or whatever believing it was a real mouse. Growing up to think a big animal like that wouldn't be dangerous. No surprise, then, that when the kids grew up they'd think piranhas and pythons and walking catfish were a good idea for pets, then go dump them in some nearby swamp or river, thinking that was *another good idea.*

And now it was as if the whole state was like those catfish, crawling up the Eastern Seaboard into North Carolina and taking over, because here in this very park there were people—people who were supposed to be in charge—who acted like bears were *pets.* Letting them wander along the roads so dumb-asses could throw marshmallows and french fries at them, like it was trick or treat and the bears weren't real bears but idiots in costumes. Doing it even after some fool had nearly had his arm torn off by a bear he was feeding from a car window, and probably would have had his arm torn off if someone in the car behind hadn't tossed out a bag of Cheetos. Denton had seen the whole bear spectacle firsthand just a month ago when he'd driven to Cherokee to see a client. The bears were actually lined up on the shoulder waiting for handouts. One had gotten out on the road in front of Denton's truck and stayed there with its big red tongue slobbering, like it was owed a meal. That was another thing the Chinese had going for them. They weren't big on pets. Hell, they *ate* their pets, or what passed for pets over here.

Denton finally saw his marker and left the trail. He paused but didn't hear anything so, if the trap had worked, maybe the creature was already dead. Denton had to admit he was relieved. If he'd caught one and it was dead, all he'd have to do was cut off the paws and do a little surgery to find the gallbladder, which shouldn't be that hard, since he'd seen the photos—greenish, shaped like a fig. If the bear hadn't died, he'd have to shoot it. He'd grown up in a place where you were supposed to enjoy being out in the woods shooting things, but he had never enjoyed being outdoors. Denton liked being able to decide how warm or cold he was going to be, and having a toilet, and knowing exactly where everything was and knowing it was close by. But here he was, way up in the woods with a pistol and knife and trap like he was Daniel frigging Boone. And what if he got caught. Having Baroque and Marlboro as lookouts probably increased the chances about a thousand percent. He'd lose a good job at the least. Maybe end up in jail, because having the gun with him meant *two* federal crimes.

But there was no bear. The store-bought ham he'd hung from the limb was gone, the trap sprung. Denton looked closer, saw two silvery-brown nails and a few hairs. The bear had leaned over the trap as if reaching over a counter. Dumb luck on the bear's part, Denton knew, but at least the damn thing might be scared enough now to think twice before going after human food again.

Screw it, Denton thought, bear, medicine, and, most of all, the brothers-in-law. Denton had eighty bucks and a credit card in his billfold. He'd take Baroque and Marlboro to the bus station in Asheville. And buy two one-way tickets to Florida. They might eventually wander back, but it'd take those two screwups months or even years to get enough money to return. Susie had sent them money to come the first time, but there was no way in hell that Denton would let that happen again.

As he began the walk back, Denton suddenly felt better than he had in a while. Everything was going to be all right. Even freezing his tail off on this mountain had been worthwhile. That was another thing the Chinese believed, or at least the Buddhists among them, that you went up a mountain to gain wisdom. And he damn sure had, finally realizing what to do about the brothers-in-law. Denton made his way back down the trail, going slow because the afternoon light was waning. He started thinking about how he'd deal with Baroque and Marlboro if they didn't want to go. Just as he decided if it came down to the pistol he wasn't above that, Denton tripped on a root and his ankle veered in one direction and the rest of his body in another. He didn't stop tumbling until he was off the trail and into the stream, ice shattering around him as he entered the tailwater of a wide, long pool face-first. Soaked from his head all the way to his waist, Denton crawled up on the bank. His teeth chattered and he could *feel* his hair turning into icicles. He knew that whatever else bad had happened in his life—embalmed wife, deadbeat bears, brothers-in-law—this was worse. A whole lot worse.

He took off his gloves and pulled out the cell phone, praying it would still work. The cell phone, unlike him, had been totally immersed, but by some kind of miracle it wasn't dead. Denton's fingers were numb but he was finally able to press the right numbers and the call went through. On the eighth ring Baroque picked up and Denton explained what had happened, or at least as best he could, because his brain was clouding with every passing second, and his words didn't match up with his thoughts the way he wanted them to. It felt like years passed before Baroque understood.

"We're coming," Baroque said. "How far from the truck are you, timewise?"

Denton didn't speak for what felt like a full minute. The connections of time and space were not so clear anymore.

"Maybe thirty minutes," he finally answered.

Denton heard Baroque speak to Marlboro, then the sound of truck doors slamming shut.

"We're on our way," Baroque said. "But we need to know if you feel cold or hot."

Denton realized that though his teeth chattered and icicles had formed in his hair he actually was, if not hot, at least warm.

"Hot," he said.

"You got to get back in the water, then," Baroque said. "You've got hypothermia. A boy on one of the shows fell in a pond and being under that cold water was all that kept him from freezing to death."

Denton tried hard to figure out if Baroque knew what he was talking about. It seemed Denton had heard of such a thing, maybe on the news, and the fact that Baroque had learned a word as long as *hypothermia*, even pronounced it correctly, struck him dimly as some kind of progress. Besides, the water would cool him off.

"You can't wait any longer," Baroque said. "In a couple of minutes you won't be able to move. We're on our way."

Denton looked at the pool, covered in ice except around the falls. Somewhere deep inside him an alarm bell went off, but it was so soft Denton couldn't figure out quite what the warning was. Baroque was still talking, telling Denton he had to do it now. Denton set the cell phone on the bank. Baroque's words were blurring. It seemed Baroque was talking real fast, though maybe that was because Denton was starting to think real slow. Breaking the ice to enter the pool seemed too much work, so Denton crawled onto the rocks above the waterfall and slid feetfirst into the pool, going in smooth as an otter.

At first they didn't see him, just the cell phone's blue-tinged screen.

"If he crawled up in the woods, he's a goner for sure," Baroque said.

Then they saw Denton hovering in the pool's center. The ice was so clear it looked like Denton was part of a magic trick.

"His eyes are open," Marlboro said.

"Of course they are," Baroque said, "and he can probably see us and hear us."

"He's not blinking."

"That's because it's like a coma, everything's shut down but his brain. His heart, I bet it's less than one beat a minute by now."

"I didn't think he'd be that blue," Marlboro said.

Baroque took a football-sized rock and threw it into the pool above Denton's head. The ice shattered, but Denton's body drifted only a few feet before it snagged on more ice.

"We'll have to go in and get him," Baroque said.

Marlboro looked at the water reluctantly.

"I guess so."

"Let me get his cell phone first," Baroque said. "He'd be mad at us if we left it. Anyway, we'd better get him to the hospital. I've been thinking more about that show. The announcer might have said fifteen minutes, not fifty. I don't guess you remember?"

Marlboro shook his head.

Baroque picked up the phone and put it in his pocket and they waded in, the water over their ankles as Baroque set his hands beneath Denton's shoulders and Marlboro lifted his feet. Once on the bank, they set Denton down. Marlboro parted his legs and positioned himself between them as if hauling a stretcher.

"His being stiff does make it easier," Marlboro said.

They made their way down the trail and arrived at the parking lot. As the day's last light fell behind the mountains, they leaned Denton against the truck.

"Should we put him in the middle?" Marlboro asked.

"We can't do that," Baroque said, "not unless you want to drive all the way to town without heat. A human can't be thawed out but once."

Baroque opened the tailgate and they slid Denton in feetfirst, placing two cinder blocks one on each side so he wouldn't shift as much. Marlboro took the lid off the Styrofoam cooler and wedged it gently, almost tenderly, under Denton's head.

"And he can still see and hear us?" Marlboro asked when they'd finished.

"Sure."

Marlboro stared at Denton.

"I can't think of anything to say to him."

They got into the cab and after a couple of tries Baroque found first gear and they made their way down the dirt road.

"He's been pretty good to us," Marlboro said. "He can be grouchy but he has let us stay with him."

"I've been thinking maybe we haven't really held up our end as much as we should have," Baroque said. "Next week I'm going over to the community college to see about that med tech degree. What we're doing helping Denton makes me feel useful."

Marlboro nodded.

"If you do that, I'll go see about an orderly job."

The road went downhill and the woods thickened. Everything was shadowy now and at the bottom of the hill was a bridge. Baroque knew from movies this was not the kind of place where anything good ever happened. A maniac or a man with a steel hook for a hand or a mutant could be hiding under the bridge. He risked shifting into second gear and found it and the truck sped up and rattled on across. Baroque let out a grateful sigh as the road rose again and the woods opened up.

"If Denton is okay, do you think they'll put us on one of the medical shows?" Marlboro asked.

"Probably," Baroque said.

"And they'll give us medals?"

"I don't know about that," Baroque said, "but if they do they should give Denton one too. The way he got himself under the ice—that was real smart."

"What do they need to get him going again?" Marlboro asked. "It doesn't have to be a special kind of hospital?"

"No, they've all been trained to do it."

"That's good," Marlboro said.

The dirt road ended at an asphalt two-lane. The truck stalled when Baroque shifted into reverse instead of neutral. He didn't try to turn the engine back on but simply stared out the windshield, unsure which way to go. Baroque looked in one direction, then the other, but he couldn't see much because it was real dark now. The headlights would have helped, but he didn't know how to turn them on.

Those Who Are Dead
Are Only Now Forgiven

The Shackleford house was haunted. In the skittering of leaves across its rotting porch, locals heard the whispered misery of ghosts. Footsteps creaked on stair boards and sobs filtered through walls. An Atlanta developer had planned to raze the house and turn the thirty acres into a retirement village. Then the economy flatlined. The house continued to fold in on itself and the meandering dirt drive became rough as a logging trail. So we'll be completely alone, Lauren had told Jody. When Jody mentioned the ghost stories, Lauren told him she'd take care of that. Leave us the hell alone, she said loudly each time they stepped inside. They'd let their eyes adjust to the house's gloaming, listening for something other than their own breathing, then spread the sleeping bag on the floor, sometimes in a bedroom but as often in the front room. He and Lauren would undress and slide into the sleeping bag and whatever chill the old house held was vanquished by the heat of their bodies.

Lauren had always spoken her mind. You're not afraid to show you are intelligent, most boys from out in the county are, Lauren had told him in their first class together. She'd asked what Jody wanted to major in at college and he said engineering. Education, she answered when asked the same question. Ninth grade was when students from upper Haywood were bused to Canton to attend the county's high school. Unlike the other boys he'd grown up with, Jody didn't fill a seat in the school's vocational wing. Instead, he entered classrooms where most of the students came from town. Their parents weren't necessarily wealthy, but they'd grown up in families where college was an expectation. As Lauren said, he'd not been afraid to show his intelligence, but first only when called on. Then he'd begun raising his hand, occasionally answering a question even Lauren couldn't answer. The teachers had encouraged him, and by spring he and Lauren both were being recommended for summer programs at Chapel Hill and Duke for low-income students.

The boys he rode the bus with no longer invited him on hunting and fishing trips. Soon they didn't bother to speak. During the long bus trip to and from school, Jody saw them staring at the books he withdrew from his backpack, not just ones for class but books Lauren passed on, tattered paperbacks of *The Catcher in the Rye* and *The Hitchhiker's Guide to the Galaxy*, books from the library on astronomy and religion. It was an act of betrayal to some. One morning near the school year's end Billy Rankin tripped Jody in the cafeteria, sent him and his tray sprawling to the floor. Billy outweighed him by fifty pounds and Jody would have done nothing if Lauren hadn't been with him. He went after Billy, driving him onto the linoleum, praying a teacher would break it up quick. But it was Lauren who got to them first. By the time a teacher intervened, Lauren had broken off two fingernails shredding Billy's left cheek.

As he left the blacktop, Jody found the dirt drive more traveled than a year ago. Less broom sedge sprouted in the packed dirt, and fresh tire prints braided the road. What's left of her is at the Shackleford place, Trey, Lauren's brother, had finally told Jody. The dirt road straightened and climbed upward. Oak trees purpled with wisteria lined both sides. Dogwoods huddled in the understory, a few last blossoms clinging to their branches. The drive curved and the trees fell away. Bedsprings appeared in a ditch, beside them a shattered porcelain toilet and a washing machine. The debris looked like a tornado's aftermath.

Each time they'd driven here their senior year, Lauren had leaned into Jody's shoulder, her hand on his thigh. Those moments had been as good as the actual lovemaking—hours alone yet awaiting them. Afterward, they stayed in the sleeping bag and made plans for what they'd do once Jody graduated from college. We'll live in a warm faraway place like Costa Rica, Lauren would say. When he said it was too bad they'd taken French, Lauren answered that learning another new language would only make it better.

More debris lay scattered on the drive and in the ditches—beer and soft drink cans, plastic garbage bags spilling contents like burst piñatas. One last curve and the Shackleford place rose before him. Next to the porch, a battered Ford Taurus appeared not so much parked as stalled in the wheel-high grass. The house's front door stood open as if he were expected.

Jody stepped onto the porch but lingered in the doorway. First he saw the TV set inside the fireplace. A rock band filled the screen but the sound was off. Shoved close to the fireplace was a bright-red couch, occupied, three faces materializing in the dusty light. The odor of meth singed the air as Jody stepped inside. Mixed and cooked by Lauren, he knew. In high school Billy and Katie Lynn hadn't attempted Chemistry I, much less the advanced courses he and Lauren passed with A's.

"Come to get the good feeling with us, Mr. College?" Billy asked.

"No," Jody said, standing beside Lauren now.

Billy pointed to a felt-lined church collection plate on the floor, among its sparse coins and bills a glass pipe and baggie.

"Well, you can at least make an offering."

Katie Lynn laughed, her voice dry and harsh.

"Come on, buddy, have a seat," Billy said, making room. "We can have us a regular high school reunion."

Jody stared at Lauren. Five months had passed since he'd last seen her. He was unsure which unsettled him more, how much beauty she'd lost or how much remained.

"I think he's still sweet on you, girl," Katie Lynn said.

Lauren looked up, her eyes glassy.

"You still sweet on me, Jody?"

He studied the room's demented furnishings. A couch and TV but no tables or chairs, the floor awash with everything from candy wrappers to a tangle of multihued Christmas lights. In a corner were some of Lauren's books, *The World's Great Religions, Absalom, Absalom*, a poetry anthology. Her computer too, its screen cracked. An orange extension cord snaked around the couch and disappeared into the kitchen. A generator, Jody realized, now hearing the machine's hum.

"Get the fire going, Billy," Lauren said, "so it'll be cozier."

He changed the disk in the DVD player and orange flames flickered on the screen. Billy's linebacker shoulders were bony now, his chest sunken.

"Want me to turn up the sound?" Billy asked.

Lauren nodded and the fireplace crackled and hissed.

"We got room for you," Katie Lynn said, patting a space between her and Lauren, but Jody remained standing.

"I want you to go with me," Jody said.

"Go where, baby?" Lauren asked.

"Back home."

"Haven't you heard?" Lauren said. "Bad girls don't get to go home. They don't even get prayed for, at least that's what Trey says."

"Then go with me to Raleigh. We'll get an apartment."

"He wants to save you from us trashy folks," Katie Lynn said, "but we ain't so bad. That collection plate, we didn't break into church and steal it. Billy bought it at the flea market."

"You ought to save us from Lauren," Billy said. "She does the cooking around here, and just look at us. We're shucking off weight like Frosty the Snowman."

"Save us, Jody," Katie Lynn said. "We're melting. We're melting."

"Come outside with me," Jody said.

Lauren followed him onto the porch. In the afternoon light he saw the yellow tinge and wondered if they were using needles too. Hepatitis was common from what he'd read on the internet. Lauren's jeans hung loose on her hips, her teeth nubbed and discolored as Indian corn. Jody imagined a breed of meth heads evolving to veins and nose and mouth, just enough flesh on bone to keep the passage-ways open.

"No one would tell me where you were," Jody said. "At least you could have."

"This is the land beyond the cell phone or internet," Lauren said. "Isn't it nice that there are a few places left where that's true?"

"You could have called from town," Jody said. "Didn't you think about what it was like for me, not knowing where you were, if you were okay?"

"Maybe I was thinking of you," Lauren said, averting her eyes. "But you've found me. Mission accomplished so now you can move on."

"Why are you doing this?" Jody asked.

The question sounded lame, like something out of a book or movie Lauren would mock.

"Oh, you know me," Lauren said. "I've never been much for delayed gratification. I find what feels good and dive right in."

"This feels good," Jody said, "living out here with those two?"

"It allows me what I need to feel good."

"What will you do when you can't get what you need?" Jody asked. "What happens then?"

"The Lord provides," Lauren said softly. "Isn't that what we learned in church? Has being around all those atheist professors caused you to lose your faith, Jody, like

Reverend Wilkinson's wife warned us about in Sunday school?"

Lauren moved closer, leaned her head lightly against his chest though her arms stayed at her sides. He smelled the meth-soured clothes, the unwashed skin and hair.

"Does being here bring back good memories?" Lauren asked.

When Jody didn't answer, she pulled her head away. Smiling, she raised her hand to his cheek. The hand was warm, blood pulsing through it yet.

"It does for me," Lauren said, and withdrew her hand. "You know I would have called or e-mailed, baby, but out here there's no signal."

"Come with me right now; don't even go back in there," Jody said. "You don't have to pack a thing. I've got money to buy you clothes, whatever else. We'll go straight to Raleigh right now."

"I can't leave, baby," Lauren said.

"Yes, you can," Jody said. "You're the one who showed me how to."

Katie Lynn came to the door.

"We need you to do some cooking, hon."

"Okay," Lauren said, and turned back to Jody. "I've got to go."

"I'll be back," he said.

Lauren paused in the doorway.

"You probably shouldn't," she said, and went on inside.

Jody got back in the truck and drove toward town. *If we make good enough grades, we can leave here,* Lauren had told him. For the first three years of high school, he and Lauren made A's in the college-prep classes. They shared the academic awards, though Lauren could have won them all if she'd wanted to. Their junior year, she made the highest SAT score in the school. That summer Lauren cashiered at Wal-Mart while Jody worked with his sister and mother at the poultry plant. He used the money for a down payment on the pickup. They'd pile it with belongings when he and Lauren left Canton for college.

In the fall of their senior year, Lauren completed the financial-aid forms Ms. Trexler, the guidance counselor, gave them. She and Jody continued to work afternoons and Saturdays, making money for what the scholarships wouldn't cover. Then one day in November Lauren told him she'd changed her mind. When neither he nor Ms. Trexler could sway her, Jody told her it was okay, that an engineer made good money, enough for them both. All Lauren had to do was wait four years and they could leave Canton forever, leave a life where checkbooks never quite balanced and repo men and pawnbrokers loomed one turn of bad luck away. Jody had watched other classmates, including many in college prep, enter such a life with an impatient fatalism. They got pregnant or arrested or simply dropped out. Some boys, more defiant, filled the junkyards with crushed metal. Crosses garlanded with flowers and keepsakes marked roadsides where they'd died. You could see it coming in the smirking yearbook photos they left behind.

Soon after he'd left for college, Lauren got fired for cursing a customer and took work at the poultry plant. Jody drove back to Canton once a month. Though phone calls and e-mails kept them connected, it seemed forever before Christmas break arrived. That first night back home, he'd picked Lauren up at her mother's house and they had gone to a party on Cove Creek. Jody expected alcohol and marijuana, some pills. What surprised him was the meth, and how casually Lauren took the offered pipe. When Billy asked if Jody wanted to try it, he shook his head. Once back at school their e-mails and phone conversations became fewer, shorter. He'd seen Lauren only once, in late January. She'd lost weight and also lost her job. At spring break, Trey told him Lauren was in Charlotte and could have no visitors. Then Jody had heard nothing.

When Jody entered Winn-Dixie, Trey was helping a customer. He finished and came over to where Jody waited. Trey offered his hand after wiping it on his stained green apron.

"So you've finished your semester?"

"Yes," Jody answered.

"I bet you made good grades, didn't you?"

Jody nodded.

"Maybe you'll inspire some kids around here to have a bit of ambition," Trey said. "What about this summer?"

"The school offered me a job in the library, but I think I'll live with Mom and slice up chickens."

"Why the hell do that?" Trey asked.

"Tuition's up again. Even with the scholarships, I'll have to get another loan. No rent and better pay if I stay here."

"They don't make it easy for a mountain boy, do they?" Trey said.

"No," Jody said.

"How's your sister?" Trey asked.

"Okay, I guess, considering."

"I heard they got Jeff for nonsupport," Trey said. "What a worthless asshole, always was. When Karen started going with him, I told her she was setting her sights way too low. You and her both tended to do that."

Trey turned to see if a customer lingered in his area.

"I went up to the Shackleford place," Jody said.

Trey grimaced.

"I knew I shouldn't have told you. I thought you had sense enough not to."

"I hadn't heard from her in over two months," Jody said.

"So now you've seen her and know not to go back," Trey said.

"Can't you do something?"

"Like what?" Trey said. "Talk to her? Pray for her? I did

that. I'm the one who went out there and got her in February, drove her to Charlotte. Three weeks, five thousand dollars. I paid half and Momma paid half."

"The law, they've got to know they're out there," Jody said. "I'd rather see her in jail than where she is."

"Six months, since they aren't dealing, Sheriff Hunnicut said, and that's with a so-called tough judge. Soon as she got out she'd be back out there."

"You can't know that," Jody said.

"Yes I can. She might have had a chance in February, but stay on that shit long as she has now and it ain't a choice. Your brain's been rewired. Besides, Hunnicut's got his hands full rounding up the ones so sorry they let their own babies breathe it, them and the ones selling to the high school kids."

"So you've given up on her, you and your momma both?" Jody asked.

"Sheriff Hunnicut told me he used to wonder why he never saw any rats inside a meth house. I mean, filth all over the place you'd expect them. Then he realized the rats were smart enough to stay clear. Think about that."

"What happened to your father at the power plant, the way it happened . . ."

Trey's face reddened.

"If she's using that as an excuse, then she's even sorrier than I thought. Momma and I had as hard a time with Daddy dying. We hold down jobs, act responsible."

"Lauren didn't say it," Jody answered. "I'm saying it."

"She had a daddy a lot longer than you did and you're doing good as anyone around here," Trey said. "That Trexler woman always put on about how smart Lauren was, such and such an IQ, such and such an SAT score. But I never saw much smarts in the decisions she made. I figured her to end up pregnant before finishing high school. Look, she'd have gotten where she is now a lot quicker if it hadn't been for you. You and me both, we've done more for her than she deserves."

A customer called for Trey to weigh some produce.

"Stay in Raleigh," Trey said. "This place is like a spider's web. You stay long enough you'll get stuck in it for good. You'll end up like her. Or me."

As he pulled out of the lot, Jody remembered the afternoon before he left for college, the last time he and Lauren went to the Shackleford house. After they'd made love, Lauren took his hand and led him upstairs, where they'd never been before. In a back bedroom were a bureau and mirror, a cardboard funeral-home fan, and a child's wooden rocking horse. Lauren had asked Jody if he knew why the house was supposedly haunted. He didn't, only that something had happened and it had been bad. As they went down the stairs, Lauren had turned to him. When I've dared them to show themselves, she had told him, I always hoped they would.

———

Supper was ready when Jody got back to his mother's house. Karen had come over with Jody's niece, Chrystal. His sister's hands were red and raw from deboning chicken carcasses and when she spoke to the child, there was harshness even when not chiding her.

"Have some corn, Jody," his mother said, lifting the bowl more with palms than fingers.

When Jody was growing up, there'd been evenings after work when his mother could barely wring a washcloth. Her fingers froze up and pain radiated from her hands to her shoulders and neck. After she'd had to quit the poultry plant and became a waitress, the pain lessened, but the fingers still curled inward.

"Hard to believe it's already May," Jody's mother said. "Just three more years and you'll be a college graduate."

"And then gone from here for good," Karen said. "Little brother always knew what he wanted. I thought I did, but I confused a hard dick for love."

"Don't talk like that," their mother said, "especially in front of a child."

"Why not, Mom?" Karen answered. "You made the same mistake."

Their mother flinched.

"Too bad you didn't knock up Lauren in high school," Karen said to Jody. "You could have taken off like Daddy did. Kept up the tradition."

"I wouldn't have done that," Jody answered.

"No?" Karen said. "I guess we'll never know, will we, little brother."

"Please," their mother said softly. "Let's talk about something else."

"Lauren didn't last long at the plant," Karen said. "A good thing. High as she was half the time, she'd have cut a hand off. Still flaunting how smart she was though. At breaks she always sat with these two Mexican women, learning to speak their jabber, helping her 'madres' fill out forms."

Chrystal reached for another biscuit and Karen slapped the child's hand. Chrystal jerked her hand back, spilled her cup of milk, and began wailing.

"See what fun you've missed out on, little brother," Karen said.

Three more years, Jody thought as he lay in bed that night. More loans to pay back and, in such an uncertain economy, perhaps no job. He remembered the Friday afternoon Ms. Trexler sat in the house's front room and explained how coming from a single-parent family would be an asset. Your son deserves a chance at a better life, Ms. Trexler had told his mother, then explained the financial-aid forms she'd brought. The guidance counselor hadn't let her gaze linger on the shabby furniture, the cracked windowpane sealed by a square of blue tarp, but her meaning was clear enough. All the while his mother had tugged nervously at her dress, her Sunday dress, as she'd listened.

Sleep would not come, so Jody pulled on his jeans and a T-shirt, went outside and sat on the porch steps. The night was cool and silent, too early for the cicadas, no trucks or cars rattling the steel bridge beyond the pasture. A quarter moon held its place among the stars. *Like a pale comma*, Lauren once said, and spoke of phases of the moon. That Friday afternoon, after all the forms had been signed, Ms. Trexler asked Jody to walk outside. Lauren has let both of us down, Ms. Trexler had said as they'd stood by her car, but don't let that keep you from achieving what you want in life.

Jody went back inside and opened his laptop. His mother didn't have internet, but he'd downloaded before-and-after photos. He watched the faces wither like flowers in time-lapsed photography. Each year appeared a decade. *Deceased* was slashed across several of the faces.

After his mother left for her shift at the diner, Jody packed a suitcase and backpack and headed into town. He went to an ATM and emptied his account, then drove on to the Shackleford house. He parked beside the Taurus and stepped up the rotting porch steps and opened the door. They were on the couch, the muted TV still flickering within the hearth.

"I want you to go to Raleigh with me," Jody said, and

stepped closer to take Lauren's hand in his. "Please, I won't ask again."

As she looked up, something sparked deep in her pupils. Something, though it wasn't indecision.

"I can't, baby," Lauren said. "I just can't."

Jody went back outside and returned with the suitcase and backpack. He set them in the center of the room and took the money from his pocket and placed it in the collection plate.

"Turn on the fire, Billy," Katie Lynn said as she filled the pipe. "This boy's been a long time out in the cold."

PART
III

PART

II

The Magic Bus

After changing out of her church clothes and helping cook noon dinner, after the table was cleared and the dishes washed and put away, Sabra went to the high pasture above the parkway to watch the cars pass. She had done it as long as she could remember. In past years her brother, Jeffrey, tagged along. They would choose any state except North Carolina and wait to see which car tag went by first. Jeffrey always picked Tennessee or Florida, so he most always won. Jeffrey had tired of the game years ago, so now Sabra went alone. A girl near sixteen is too old for such nonsense, her mother had said in June, but Sabra kept coming. Sunday afternoon was her only free time and she'd spend it however she liked.

She heard the truck's engine and looked down at the farmhouse. Her parents and Jeffrey were headed to Boone for an ice cream and then on to Valle Crucis to visit Aunt Corrie for news about Sabra's first cousin Jim, who was in Vietnam. They'd be back around six, but before then Sabra would need to start supper. Dust billowed behind the pickup until the county road dead-ended at a gray wooden sign that said BLUE RIDGE PARKWAY. The truck turned left, passed the pull-off and its picnic table, and disappeared. Sabra sat down and pulled her knees to her chest. Cars went by in a steady procession, which was no surprise, since it was two days before the Fourth.

One tag blurred into the next, but Sabra always knew the state. A few were tricky, especially North Carolina and Tennessee, which were white with black letters and numbers, but even then she could tell them apart. But Sabra hardly paid those any mind. It was the far places like New Mexico or California or Alaska, whose tags had blues and golds and reds in them, that she looked for. Each time one passed she imagined what it would be like to live there instead of a gloomy farm where days dripped by slow as molasses and she did the same thing all week beginning at daylight milking a cow and ending at night putting up the supper dishes. Even Sundays, the best day, since her father didn't make her and Jeffrey do farmwork, mornings were spent hearing about the world's wickedness, how everything from drive-in theaters to rock music was the devil's doing.

Once September came and school started back up,

things wouldn't be much better. Sheila Blankenship, Sabra's best friend since third grade, had quit school in May to get married. There would still be afternoon and weekend chores, including, come fall, harvesting the tobacco, the hardest and nastiest job there was. Resin not even Lava soap got off would stain her hands and gum her hair, have to be cut out with scissors.

Sabra had seen thirty-seven states when the minibus lurched into view. Flowers of different sizes and colors had been painted on the sides and top. On the back window, in large purple letters, were the words *The Magic Bus*. The minibus made it to the pull-off and sputtered to a halt. Two women got out. The taller one opened the hood and both women disappeared as steam billowed out. When the haze cleared, they and the minibus were still there. The radiator would need water, Sabra knew. She hesitated only a few moments before she stood and dusted off her blue jeans, walked down to the house, and took a milk pail from the porch.

As she came down the slope onto parkway land, Sabra saw that it wasn't two women but a woman and a man, both with long hair. The woman, who didn't look much older than Sabra, wore a loose-fitting brown dress made of soft leather. She wore no bra or makeup, but her neck was adorned with strands of beads. The man was older. He wore a red bandanna, ragged blue jeans, and a green army shirt with cutoff sleeves. A button pinned on the shirt's lapel said

Feed Your Head. He'd not used a razor for a while. Hippies, that's what they were called, though her father used worse names when he saw them on TV. Sabra stopped at the edge of the pull-off.

They were both barefoot but this hadn't stopped the woman from wandering into a blackberry patch, her fingers stained by berries she dropped in a paper cup. The woman hummed to herself as she moved to another bush. The man stood beside the minibus.

"You ain't supposed to pick them," Sabra said.

The woman turned and smiled.

"Why not?" she asked softly.

"The park ranger says because it's federal land."

"That's all the more reason we should be able to pick them," the man said, looking at her now. "This land belongs to the people."

Like the woman's voice, his voice had a flatness about it, like the newsmen on TV. Sabra shifted the milk pail to her other hand.

"I'm just saying it so you'll know," she said. "That ranger comes by most every hour."

A station wagon passing the PICNIC AREA sign flicked on its turn signal, slowed, then sped up. Children's faces crowded the backseat's passenger window, their eyes wide.

"Better than seeing a bear, scarier too, at least for Mom

and Pop," the man said, watching the station wagon disappear around a curve.

The woman came out of the blackberry patch and offered the cup to Sabra.

"Have some," she said.

"You can come closer, we're harmless," the man said, and walked over to stand beside the woman. "Like the song says, we're just groovin' on a Sunday afternoon."

"Okay," Sabra said, and stepped nearer.

The woman shook five berries into Sabra's free hand, did the same for the man. The berries were full ripe and their juice sweetened Sabra's mouth.

"My name is Wendy," the woman said when they'd eaten the berries, "and this is Thomas."

"I'm Sabra, Sabra Norris. I live across the ridge."

"*Sabra*, what a beautiful name," Wendy said.

"Very exotic sounding," the man said.

"Anyway," Sabra said. "I figured you to need this pail. There's a creek yonder side of the parkway."

"Where?" Thomas asked, taking the pail.

Sabra pointed to a stand of birch trees.

"That's kind of you," Wendy said. "The best thing about being on the road is meeting so much love and goodness."

Thomas crossed the parkway and went into the woods. Wendy sat on the pull-off's curb, motioned for Sabra to join her.

"My cousin Jim is in the army," Sabra said. "Was Thomas?"

Wendy looked puzzled.

"Oh, you mean his shirt?"

"Yes," Sabra said.

"No, Thomas is into peace, not war."

"He must have got a high lottery number," Sabra said. "Jim's was thirty-two."

"Thomas is thirty years old," Wendy said, "so he was before the lottery. They still had a draft but he didn't get picked. Is your cousin in Vietnam?"

"Yes," Sabra said.

"Why wasn't he a conscientious objector?" Wendy asked.

"What's that?"

"It means you don't believe in hurting other people, especially in a war we shouldn't be in."

"I guess Jim figured it his duty," Sabra said, "same as when Uncle Jesse went to World War Two and my daddy went to Korea."

"Well, I hope we get out of Vietnam soon," Wendy said. "That way your cousin and all the rest can come home."

A car hauling a silver trailer went by, a line of cars behind it. Several drivers stared as they passed. Probably figure I'm with Wendy and the bus, Sabra thought. The notion pleased her, and she wished that she wasn't wearing a checked two-pocket cowgirl shirt.

"He must miss being away from this place," Wendy said. "It's so beautiful here."

"It's not always so pretty," Sabra answered. "Lots of times there's fog so thick it feels like you're being smothered, and the rain can last for days. Summer's the only time you get days like this."

"San Francisco's like that too," Wendy said, "but I love those gray days. It's like the world wraps a soft blanket around the city. It makes you feel cozy, safe and snug. On mornings like that Thomas and I will stay in bed half the day."

Sabra glanced at Wendy's left hand.

"Have you known Thomas a long time?"

"A year come this September," Wendy said.

"How did you meet?"

"My first semester of college I took a long walk one Sunday, just to see the city. It was obvious I didn't know my way around. Thomas came up to me and volunteered to be my guide."

"So you didn't grow up there?"

"Missouri."

"Do you still go to college?" Sabra asked.

"No," Wendy said. "I'm learning a lot more from being with Thomas."

"Like what?"

"How people need to do things instead of just talking about doing them. Like this trip. One day Thomas said we should do it and two hours later we were on the road."

Thomas came out of the woods, the pail in his right

hand. As he crossed, water sloshed over the rim, darkened the parkway's gray asphalt.

"You need help, babe?" Wendy asked, shifting her hands to rise from the curb, but Thomas shook his head.

"I've never gone anywhere," Sabra said. "The only time I've even been out of North Carolina was a school trip to Knoxville."

"Your family never goes on vacations?" Wendy asked.

"Me and my brother, Jeffrey, have been begging to go to Florida long as I can remember," Sabra said, "but my parents say we don't have the money."

"You don't need money, not much at least," Wendy said. "Thomas and I had fifty dollars when we left San Francisco six weeks ago."

"But how do you eat, or buy gas?"

"You share things," Wendy said, and touched the beads on her neck. "I make some of these every day. People give me money for them, or food, even gas. Thomas, he has things to share too."

Sabra looked west toward Grandfather Mountain. The sun had settled on the summit where, like a fishing bobber, it waited to be tugged under. Her parents and Jeffrey had probably already left Aunt Corrie's. Time to head back across the pasture, but Sabra didn't want to. She wished the bus had come earlier, right after her family left.

Thomas slammed the hood shut and walked over to the curb but did not sit down. He held the pail out to Sabra and she rose from the curb to take it. Wendy got up too and Thomas wrapped an arm around her waist, pulled her close, and kissed her on the cheek.

"We're good to go, baby," he said.

"But it's so nice here," Wendy said. "Let's stay for the night."

"A nice place it is," Thomas answered, "but what about food, my lady?"

"We have enough bread and peanut butter left for a sandwich."

Thomas groaned.

"We've got eighteen dollars. I was thinking we could stop in Boone and get a real meal."

"I can get you a real meal," Sabra said, "and it won't cost you anything."

"What a kind thing for you to offer," Wendy said.

"What about your parents?" Thomas asked. "They might not like your doing that for strangers, especially ones who look like us."

"I won't let them know," Sabra said. "They go to bed soon as it gets dark. You can have chicken, green beans, and corn bread, and I'll make some potato salad. I can bring you fresh milk too."

"That's worth waiting a few hours for," Thomas said.

"But you'd have to bring it all here," Wendy said, "and in the dark."

"You could meet me in the barn," Sabra said. "I can show

you where it is. Once it starts to get near dark, you can come there."

"How will we get back here?" Thomas said. "We don't have a flashlight."

"I'll get one you can use, or you can spend the night in the barn. Come morning, I'm the one that does the milking."

"We like being outside and seeing the stars," Thomas said, "but the food part, that sounds good."

"Are you sure it will be okay?" Wendy asked.

"I really want to," Sabra answered. "Like you said, it's good to share what you have."

Smiling, Wendy reached out and touched Sabra's cheek, let the hand stay a few moments. Sabra felt the warmth in the hand.

"You would love San Francisco, Sabra," Wendy said, "and it would love you."

There was only time to make the potato salad before Sabra's family returned. Jeffrey rushed in, grabbed his ball glove, and ran back outside as her parents entered the house.

"You go visiting and that boy gets like a coiled spring," Sabra's mother said.

"That's how a twelve-year-old boy should act," her father said. "I'd not want a son who acted different."

They could hear the ball thumping against the wood-shed now.

"Dammit, that reminds me," her father said. "I need to fill the spray tanks for tomorrow."

He went back out the door. The ball stopped thumping for a few moments, then resumed. Her mother came into the kitchen and put on an apron.

"You look to have been dawdling, girl."

"I decided to make potato salad," Sabra said. "It took longer than I thought."

"Well, nothing to fret over," her mother said. "That ice cream will keep your daddy and brother from getting cranky."

While her mother floured and fried the chicken, Sabra put the beans on, mixed the corn bread, and placed it in the oven.

"How's Aunt Corrie?" Sabra asked.

"Fine except she's got this notion that Jim won't come home alive."

"Why does she think that?"

"Because of that second boy from Valle Crucis getting killed over there," her mother said. "Death always comes in threes, that's what she told your daddy and me."

Sabra grimaced.

"What is that look for?" her mother asked.

"It just seems everyone around here always expects the worst," Sabra said.

"I don't know that to be true," her mother said. "Anybody would have worries if their child was over there."

"Jim doesn't have to be there," Sabra said softly. "He could tell the army he's not wanting to fight anymore. He could be a conscientious objector."

Her mother stopped forking the fried chicken onto paper towels.

"Lord, girl, don't let your daddy hear you talk like that. You know how he gets just hearing about such things on the news. No need for his own daughter to rile him up more, especially when he's been extra sweet to you today."

"How?" Sabra asked.

"Your birthday present," her mother said. "I'm letting the cat out of the bag, but it's only five more days so I'll tell you. We went by Kmart and bought that record player you've been wanting."

"But you all said it was too expensive," Sabra said.

"Your daddy argued we should figure in a couple of dollars for all the ice cream you've missed this summer. Anyway, it looks to be a good year for us. All that June rain will get us through this dry spell. We'll have that barn filled with hay and curing tobacco come fall."

Sabra's mother poured the last of the grease into an old coffee can, turned, and smiled.

"See, that's not expecting the worst, is it?"

"No, I guess not," Sabra said.

"Then put a smile on your face and call your daddy and brother in to eat, and don't let on you know about that record player. He wanted it to be a surprise."

———

Once all the farmhouse lights were out, Sabra took the flashlight from under her pillow. She took off her bra and put on an orange T-shirt with TENNESSEE on the front, quietly made her way to the kitchen, and filled a grocery bag. How she'd explain the missing food tomorrow, Sabra did not know. Probably won't need to explain it, she told herself, but I'm at least going to go see.

Sabra eased out the front door and headed to the barn, the porch's bare bulb, and habit, guiding her. She was almost to the barn mouth when she saw the small orange glow, thought it a lightning bug until she turned on the flashlight. Thomas sat on the barn floor, his back against a stable door. Wendy sat a few feet away. A bright-yellow backpack lay between them.

"Daddy don't allow lit cigarettes in the barn," Sabra said.

Thomas smiled.

"Well, it's not a cigarette, at least the kind he's thinking about."

The orange tip glowed as Thomas inhaled. After a few moments, he pursed his lips and let the smoke whisper out of his mouth. He passed what was in his hand to Wendy, who did the same thing.

"You ever smoked a joint?" Thomas asked.

Sabra shook her head and looked back toward the farmhouse. If the marijuana's odor lingered long enough, her father would smell it. It won't, Sabra told herself. You're just thinking the worst.

"You don't look like you much approve of it," Thomas said.

"I've heard what it does to you."

"Good things or bad?" Thomas asked, and took the joint from Wendy.

"Bad," Sabra said.

Thomas exhaled again, let the smoke haze the air between them.

"And who told you that?"

"My health teacher," Sabra said.

Thomas raised the joint and made a slow swirling motion as if writing something in the air.

"You think he's ever gotten stoned?"

Sabra tried to imagine gray-haired Mr. Borders, who was a church deacon and didn't even smoke cigarettes, inhaling and holding the marijuana smoke in his lungs, letting it out slow like Thomas and Wendy did.

"No," Sabra said.

"Then he doesn't know, does he?" Thomas said.

"I guess not," Sabra said, freeing a horse blanket from a nail.

The joint was just a stub now, hardly enough left to hold. Thomas brought it to his mouth a last time and laid what was left on his pants leg, rubbed it into the cloth with his palm.

"All gone," he said, raising the hand.

Sabra set down the grocery bag on the horse blanket, positioned the flashlight to cast the light before them. She took out two forks and two paper plates, then the Tupperware bowl and quart jar of milk.

"I'm sorry I couldn't heat it up for you," Sabra said, "and I didn't bring cups."

Thomas placed corn bread and chicken on his plate, forked out some potato salad. He took a big bite out of the chicken.

"Damn, that's good," he said, and pointed his fork at Wendy. "You had better dig in now or there will be nothing left."

"What about you, Sabra?" Wendy asked.

"I ate plenty at supper," Sabra said, and lifted the jar of milk from the bag. "I didn't have room for cups, but I figured you'd not mind about that."

Though some milk remained in the jar, the Tupperware bowl was soon empty except for a few bones.

"The radiator boiling over was the best thing that could have happened," he said.

"It was," Wendy agreed. "We'd have passed right by and never known a new friend was just over the hill."

"Maybe it was meant to be," Thomas said, meeting Sabra's eyes. "Things happen for a reason. What's that quote you like so much, Wendy, the one about destiny."

"We don't find our destiny, it finds us," Wendy answered.

"I believe that," Thomas said, still looking at Sabra. "Don't you?"

"I guess so," Sabra said.

Thomas settled his head against the stall door, his eyes half closed. Wendy opened the backpack and brought out a strand of beads like the ones she wore and gave it to Sabra.

"I made these for you while we waited."

"They're as pretty as anything I've ever seen, even a rainbow," Sabra said. "Thank you so much."

She held the beads in both hands, slowly stretched the elastic, and let them tighten around her neck.

"Do they look good on me?" Sabra asked.

"They look divine, but two strands would look even better," Wendy said. "You want to make one yourself? It's easy."

"Okay."

Sabra moved closer, crossed her legs the same way Wendy did. Wendy set a spool of elastic and a plastic bag of beads between them. Sabra picked up a piece of string, watched Wendy tie a double-knot an inch from one end and did the same. She began sifting beads from the plastic bag, trying to find one of each color.

"You can do it that way," Wendy said, "but it's better if you let the colors surprise you, like this."

Wendy reached into the plastic bag and pulled out a single green bead. She placed it on the string and, again without looking, brought up an orange one. Sabra did the same thing.

"They do look prettier this way," Sabra said when she'd finished. "I guess people do this all the time in San Francisco, make things I mean."

Wendy smiled.

"They do."

"What else do they do there?" Sabra asked.

"Sing and dance, look after each other, love each other."

"Get stoned," Thomas said, his eyes fully open now. He laid a hand on Wendy's thigh, caressed it a moment, and removed his hand. "Make love, not war."

"And everybody's young," Wendy said. "You have to go there to believe it."

"I want to go there someday," Sabra said.

"Then one day you will," Wendy said, "and once you get there, you will never want to leave."

"Well, when I do," Sabra said, "the first people I'll look for are you all."

"Of course," Wendy said. "You can stay with us until you find a pad of your own, can't she, Thomas?"

"Sure," Thomas said, "but why wait when you can hitch a ride on the magic bus."

At first Sabra thought Thomas was joking, but he wasn't grinning or even cracking a smile. Wendy wasn't grinning either. Sabra thought about what it would be like once Thomas and Wendy left. She'd see no one near her age until Sunday. But even then it would be the same people and they'd be talking about the same things and in the same way.

"You mean go with you?" Sabra asked. "Tomorrow, I mean?"

"Tomorrow or even tonight," Thomas said.

"I would like to go with you," Sabra said softly, wanting to pretend a bit longer that she actually might.

"You would be welcome," Wendy said, "but it might be better if you waited awhile. I mean, how old are you?"

"Seventeen."

Thomas looked at Wendy.

"Hell, you were just a year older when I found you. A lot of girls out there are as young or younger. This is what it's all about, babe, being free while you're young enough to realize what freedom is."

"I guess so," Wendy said.

Thomas nodded at the strand of beads coiled in Sabra's palm.

"Why don't you try them on," he said.

Sabra slipped the beads over her head, tugged at them so they settled next to the other strand. She thought about what her father would say if he saw them on her. Or her mother, she'd not like them either. Thomas sifted more marijuana onto the smoking papers, twisted the ends.

"What's it really like then?" Sabra asked. "The marijuana, I mean?"

"Like dreaming, except you're awake," Thomas said.

"But only good dreams," Wendy added, "the kind you want to have."

"But it doesn't hurt you?" Sabra asked, looking at Wendy.

"No," Wendy said. "It helps heal you, makes the bad things go away."

Thomas lit the joint and held it out to Sabra.

"You can try it if you like, or I've got some serious mind candy."

He reached into his pocket and pulled out an aspirin bottle, the label half torn away. Inside were round pink tablets mixed with blue-and-red capsules the shape of .22 shorts.

Sabra took the joint.

"Breathe in and hold it in your lungs as long as you can," Thomas said.

"Not too long at first," Wendy cautioned, "because it will make you cough."

Sabra did what they said, stifled a cough, and handed the joint back to Thomas, who took two quick draws, exhaled. They'd passed the joint around twice more before Thomas reached out his free hand, twined a portion of Wendy's hair around a finger. He pulled his finger back slowly, hair tugging the scalp a moment before he let the hair slip free.

"Come here, baby."

Thomas inhaled and Wendy moved closer, let the smoke funnel into her mouth.

"Now you," Thomas said.

When Sabra didn't move, he slid over to her.

"Open your mouth," Thomas said.

She shut her eyes, did what he asked, felt his warm smoky breath in her throat and lungs. As Thomas's breath expired, his lips brushed hers.

Thomas pushed himself back against the stall door, took a long final draw, and rubbed the residue into his jeans. Wendy covered her face with both hands. She giggled, then lifted her hands to reveal a wide grin.

"I am soo stoned."

"I told you it was good shit," Thomas said.

"It is good," Sabra agreed, though she felt no difference except a dryness in the throat.

"If we had brought the transistor we could dance," Wendy said.

"I doubt they play much Quicksilver or Dead around here, baby," Thomas said. "Motown either."

Sabra thought of the record player, but even if she'd had some 45s there'd be no place to plug it in.

Wendy's face brightened.

"I can hum songs, though. That will be almost as good. I'll be like a jukebox and play anything we want."

Wendy moved the flashlight so that it shone toward the barn's center. She stood and placed a hand around Thomas's upper arm.

"Come on," she said.

Thomas got up and Wendy pressed her head against his chest.

"What song do you want, babe?"

" 'White Rabbit,' " Thomas said.

Wendy began to hum and she and Thomas swayed side to side, their feet barely moving. Sabra wished she had some water for her parched throat. She was reaching for the milk when it happened. Thomas and Wendy, the barn, the night itself slid back a ways and then returned, except everything felt off plumb. For a few moments all Sabra felt was panic. She closed her eyes and tried to block out everything except Wendy's humming. Soon the humming seemed as much inside of her as outside. Sabra felt it even in her fingertips, a pleasant tingling. When she opened her eyes, it did feel like a dream, a warm good dream. She watched Thomas and Wendy dance, holding each other so close together. They were in love and not afraid to show it. Never had anything so beautiful, so wondrous, ever happened on this farm. Never.

Wendy stopped humming but still pressed her head against Thomas's chest.

"What song now?" Wendy asked.

"I don't care," Thomas said, "but Sabra should get a dance too."

"Yes," Wendy agreed.

"I don't think I can," Sabra said. "I'm dizzy."

Thomas went over and helped Sabra to her feet, steadied her a moment, and led her to the barn's center.

"What song do you want, Sabra?" Wendy asked.

"I don't know," she answered. "You pick one."

"I'll do 'Both Sides Now,'" Wendy said. "It's a pretty song."

Wendy sat by the stall door and began to hum. Thomas put his arm around Sabra's waist and pulled her close. She let her head lie against his chest like Wendy had. A few times she and Sheila had pretended to dance, copying couples on television who glided across ballrooms, but this was easier. You just leaned into each other and moved your feet a little. A part of her seemed to watch from somewhere else as she and Thomas danced, close yet far away at the same time. She could smell Thomas, musky but not so bad. He leaned his face closer to hers.

"Someone as lovely as you has to have a boyfriend."

"No," Sabra said, not adding that her parents wouldn't allow her to date yet.

"I find that hard to believe," Thomas said, "just as hard to believe that you're really seventeen. How old are you, really?"

"Sixteen."

"Sweet sixteen," Thomas said. "That's old enough."

He placed his free hand against her back, brought Sabra even closer, her breasts flattening against his chest. The hand on her waist resettled where spine and hip met, all of her pressed into him now. She could feel him through the denim. Their feet no longer moved and only their hips swayed. Sabra looked over at Wendy, whose eyes were closed as she hummed the last few notes.

"What song do you two want next?" Wendy asked.

Sabra slipped free of Thomas's embrace. The barn wobbled a few moments and she had to stare at her sneakers, the straw and dirt under them, to keep her balance. When the barn resettled it had shrunk, especially the barn mouth.

"It's your turn, Wendy," Sabra said.

Wendy opened her eyes.

"I've had him all day, so you get him now."

Thomas settled a hand on Sabra's upper arm.

"Wendy doesn't mind sharing," he said.

"I'm dizzy," Sabra said, "too dizzy to dance anymore."

Thomas nodded, let his hand slide down her inner arm, his fingers brushing over her palm.

"That's fine," Thomas said. "The first time you do things, it's always a bit scary. It was the same for Wendy."

"So another dance with me, baby?" Wendy asked. "Or is it time to unplug the jukebox?"

"Time to unplug the jukebox," Thomas said. "Time to get back on the road."

"I thought you were staying until morning," Sabra said.

"This bus has no set schedule," Thomas said. "When it comes by, you either get on board or you're left behind."

Wendy put the elastic and beads in the backpack and tightened the straps. She stood up, a bit unsteadily, and walked over to the barn mouth.

"So," Thomas said, staring at Sabra, "ready to get on the bus?"

"I want to go, it's just . . ." Sabra paused. "I mean, I was thinking maybe you all could give me your address, or a phone number. That way I can find you."

"But you're coming," Thomas said, locking his eyes on hers. "It's just that you're not sure you should leave tonight."

"Yes," Sabra said. "That's what I mean."

"The moon has turned sideways and is making a smiley face," Wendy said, "really and truly."

Thomas picked up the flashlight and leaned against a stall. He let the beam shine on the floor between him and Sabra. She could barely make out his face.

"Sometimes if you're chained," Thomas said, "other people have to set you free."

"I'm not chained," Sabra said.

"If that were true, you'd leave right now," Thomas said. "I can teach every part of you how to be free, your mind and your body."

"I've got to go," Sabra said.

A match flared. Thomas slowly lowered the match into the stall. His hand came back up empty.

"Like I said, sometimes it takes someone else to set you free."

"That's not funny," Sabra said. "I think you need to leave too."

"Come see the smiley face," Wendy said.

Sabra heard the fire first, a crackling inside the stall, but she didn't believe it until she smelled smoke. Flames began licking through the stall slats. Sabra snatched the horse blanket from the barn floor, was about to the open the stall door when Thomas's arm stopped her.

"Come on," he said. "We've got to leave."

"No," Sabra shouted, and tore herself free.

She opened the stall door and swatted at the flames, but they had already leaped into the next stall. The blanket caught fire and she couldn't put it out. The fire climbed into the loft and soon Sabra could barely see through the smoke. She stumbled out of the barn. Smoke wadded like cotton in her lungs and she coughed all the way to the spring trough. The farmhouse lights were on and her father was running toward the barn, Jeffrey and her mother trailing behind. In the high pasture she saw a beam of light pause where the fence was, then move onto parkway land and disappear.

Sabra didn't know if she had slept or not, but she was awake when the dark in the east began to lighten. Her mother came into her room a few minutes later and told Sabra that barn or no barn, the cow would need to be milked. Sabra got dressed. When she passed through the front room, her father was asleep on the couch, still in his overalls. Soot grimed his face and hands and he smelled of smoke. The black patch where the barn had been yet smoldered, the milk pail nearby, lying on its side. The cow was drinking at the spring trough and looked up as Sabra walked by. She went on past the charred ground and into the high pasture and slipped through the fence.

The bus wasn't there, but the flashlight was in the grass by the curb. She switched it off and made her way back up the slope and into the high pasture. Below, the cow had left the spring trough and stood by the barn's ashes, waiting to be milked, not knowing where else to go.

The Dowry

After Mrs. Newell took away his plate and coffee cup, Pastor Boone lingered at the table and watched the thick flakes fall. The garden angel's wings were submerged, the redbud's dark branches damasked white. Be grateful it's not stinging sleet, Pastor Boone told himself as Mrs. Newell returned to the rectory's dining room.

"You'll catch the ague if you go out in such weather," the housekeeper said, and nodded at his Bible. "Instead of hearing yourself read the Good Book, you'll be hearing it read over your coffin."

"Hear it, Mrs. Newell?" Pastor Boone smiled. "Do you dispute church doctrine that the dead remain so until Christ's return?"

"Pshaw," the housekeeper said. "You know my meaning."

Pastor Boone nodded.

"Yes, we could wish for a better day, but I promised I would come."

"Another week won't matter," the housekeeper said. "Youthful folk have all the time in the world."

"It's been eight months, Mrs. Newell," he reminded her, "and, alas, they are not so youthful, especially Ethan. Two years of war took much of his youth from him, perhaps all."

"I still say they can wait another week," the housekeeper said. "Maybe by then the Colonel will die of spite and cap a snuffer on all this fuss."

"I worry more that in a week Ethan will be the one harmed," Pastor Boone replied, "and by his own volition."

The housekeeper let out an exasperated sigh.

"Let me fetch Mr. Newell to hitch the horse and drive you out there."

"No, it's Sunday," Pastor Boone said. "If he'll ready the buggy, that's enough. The solitude will allow me to reflect on next week's sermon."

The snow showed no signs of letting up as he released the brake handle, but the buggy's canvas roof kept the snow off him, and the overcoat's thick wool provided enough warmth. The wheels shushed through the town's trodden snow. There were no other sounds, the storefronts shuttered and yards and porches empty; the only signs of habitation were windows lambent with hearth light. He passed Noah Andrews's house. The physician would scold him for being out in such inhospitable weather, but Noah, also in his seventies, would do the same if summoned. Above, a low sky dulled to the color of lead. An appropriateness in that, Pastor Boone thought.

When the war had begun five years ago, he had watched as families who'd lived as good neighbors, many kin somewhere in their lineage, became implacable enemies. Fistfights occurred and men carried rifles to church services, though at least, unlike in other parts of the county, no killing had occurred within the community. Instead, local men died at Cold Harbor and Stones River and Shiloh, which in Hebrew, he'd told Noah Andrews, meant "place of peace." The majority of the church's congregants sided with the Union, those men riding west to join Lincoln's army in Tennessee, but some, including the Davidsons, joined the Secessionists. Pastor Boone's sympathies were with the Union as well, though no one other than Noah Andrews knew so. To hold together what frayed benevolence remained in the church, a pastor need appear neutral, he'd told himself. Yet there were times he suspected his silence had been mere cowardice.

Now Ethan Burke, who fought for the Union, wanted to marry Colonel Davidson's daughter, Helen. The couple had come to him before last week's service, once again pleading for his help. They had known each other all their lives, been baptized in the French Broad by Pastor Boone on the same spring Sunday. When Ethan and Helen were twelve, they'd asked if he'd marry them when they came of age. The adults had been amused. Since the war's end last spring, Pastor Boone had watched them talking together before and after church, seen their quick touches. But when Ethan called on Helen at the Davidsons' farm, the Colonel met him at the door, a Colt pistol in his remaining hand. You'll not step on this porch again and live, he'd vowed. Ethan and Helen had taken Colonel Davidson at his word. Every Sunday afternoon for eight months Ethan, whose family owned only a swaybacked mule, walked three miles to the Davidson farm and did the chores most vexing for a one-handed man. While Helen watched from the porch, Ethan replaced the barn's warped boards and rotting shingles, cleaned out the well, and stacked hay bales in the loft. Afterward, he stood on the steps and talked to Helen until darkness began settling over the valley. Then he'd walk back to the farmhouse where his widowed mother and younger siblings awaited him.

The congregants who'd fought Union seemed ready to leave the war behind them, even Reece Triplett, who'd lost two brothers at Cold Harbor, but not Colonel Davidson, nor his nephew and cousin, who'd served under the Colonel in the North Carolina Fifty-Fifth. Easier for the victors than the vanquished to forgive, Pastor Boone knew. Colonel Davidson sat stone-faced through the sermons, and unlike Ethan and the other veterans, including his own kinsmen, the Colonel wore his butternut field coat to every service. When Pastor Boone suggested that it was time to put the uniform away, Colonel Davidson nodded at the empty sleeve. Some things don't let you forget, Pastor, he had replied brusquely. Give me back a hand and I'll be ready to forgive, as your Bible says.

Ethan had been there that Sunday, and knew, just as Pastor Boone knew, that the man was serious. Even before the war, Colonel Davidson had been a hard man, quick to take offense at the least slight. Once a peddler quipped that Davidson's stallion looked better suited for plowing and it took the sheriff and two other men to keep him from thrashing the fellow. A hard man made harder by four years of watching men die all around him, and, of course, the hand cleaved by grapeshot. But others had suffered too. Pastor Boone had seen it in the faces of old and young alike. He had witnessed families grieving, sometimes brought news of the death himself. Those who didn't have men in the war endured their share of fear and deprivation as well. Hardships he himself had been spared. Even in the war's brutal last winter, he had never lacked firewood and food, and, childless, no son to fear for. No outliers had abused him. Almost alone in that dark time, he, Christ's shepherd, had been blessed.

The horse's nostrils exhaled white plumes, its hooves gaining cautious purchase on the slopes. A breeze came up and the snow slanted. Cold slipped under the pastor's collar, between buttons. Faint boot prints appeared in the snow. As the prints deepened, Pastor Boone made out where hobnails secured a heel, newspaper replaced worn-out leather. The youth had endured this trek while Davidson sat inside his warm farmhouse. Pastor Boone reconsidered next Sunday's sermon. Instead of a chapter from Acts on mercy, he pondered the opening verse in Obadiah, *The pride of thine own heart hath deceived thee.*

The boot prints continued to deepen, and the horse followed them toward a smudge of chimney smoke. As the buggy crossed a creek, ice crackled beneath the wheels. An elopement to Texas would have been what many other couples would do, but Ethan, whose father had died of smallpox in the war's final year, would not countenance being so far from his mother and siblings. The land bottomed out and the woods fell away. Pastor Boone passed corn and hay fields drowsing under the snow, awaiting spring.

Ethan was leaving the woodshed with an armload of kindling. He came to the porch edge, set the kindling beside three thick hearth logs, and returned to the shed. Helen stood on the porch, bundled in a woolen cloak and scarf. When she saw the buggy, Helen called out toward the shed. Ethan emerged, an axe gripped in his right hand. As the buggy halted in the yard, Colonel Davidson's stern visage appeared at the window, withdrew. Ethan leaned the axe against the shed and tethered the horse to a fence post. He helped Pastor Boone down from the seat, then fetched water for the horse as Pastor Boone went up on the porch. Helen took his free hand with one equally cold.

"We didn't know if you would come," she said, "what with the weather so bad."

The door opened and Mrs. Davidson appeared with a cup of coffee.

"Welcome, Pastor," Mrs. Davidson said, and turned to Helen. "Give this to Ethan, Daughter."

Helen took the cup and handed it to Ethan, who waited on the steps.

"Come in, Pastor Boone," Mrs. Davidson said, "and you, Daughter, you should come in as well, at least a few minutes."

"Unless Ethan comes, I'm staying on the porch," Helen replied, "but we *will* hear what is said."

As Pastor Boone stepped inside, Helen's firm hand on the jamb ensured the door remained ajar. Mrs. Davidson took his overcoat and disappeared into a back room. Dim as the afternoon was outside, the parlor was gloamier. What light the fireplace offered slowly unshrouded the room—a painting of a hunter and his dog, a burgundy rug, a settee and bookshelf, last, in the far corner, a Windsor armchair occupied by the Colonel. The patriarch gave the slightest acknowledgment and remained seated. Brown yet lingered in the gray swept-back hair. Though Davidson was a decade younger, Pastor Boone never felt older in his presence.

Mrs. Davidson returned from the back room with a cup of coffee.

"Here, Pastor."

Pastor Boone took it gratefully because the cold sliced through the half-open door, tamped what heat the fire offered. He raised the cup to his mouth, blew slowly so the moist warmth glazed his cheeks and brow. He sipped and nodded approvingly.

"It's ever a blessing to drink real coffee again," Mrs. Davidson said. "We were long enough without it."

The Colonel shifted in his chair, his gaze locking on Pastor Boone's Bible.

"Am I to assume your visit is in an official capacity?"

"I come at the request of your daughter and Ethan," Pastor Boone replied, "but I also come as a friend to everyone here, including you."

"That door needs to be shut," Colonel Davidson told his wife.

"Don't do it, Mother," Helen said from the porch. "We'll hear what is said."

Pastor Boone allowed himself a slight smile. He was tempted to speak of Helen being much her father's child, decided it prudent not to. Mrs. Davidson stared at the floor.

"Very well," Colonel Davidson said. "The chill can hasten us past civilities. Have your say, Pastor."

"It is time for all of us to heal, Leland," Pastor Boone said.

"Heal," Colonel Davidson answered, and lifted his left

arm. "As your friend Doctor Andrews can inform you, there are things that cannot be healed."

"Not by man perhaps," Pastor Boone said, raising the Bible, "but by God, by his grace. Colossians says *Forgive as the Lord forgave you*."

"So you have come to bandy verses," the Colonel said, tugging back the sleeve so firelight reddened the stubbed wrist. "*Life shall go for life, eye for eye, tooth for tooth*, thus hand for a hand."

"Luke says *love your enemies, do good to them*."

"Leviticus says to chase our enemies," Colonel Davidson countered, "*and they shall fall before you by the sword*."

"You quote overly from the Old Testament," Pastor Boone said. "Therein lies more retribution than forgiveness."

"Yet they are cleaved together as one book," Colonel Davidson answered. "Thus we choose which verses to live by."

"Ethan has suffered as well," Pastor Boone said. "You have lost a hand, he has lost his youth. What you saw on the battlefield, he saw. What anger, what hatred you felt toward the enemy, he felt also."

"I accept his hatred now no less than then."

"But he doesn't hate you," Pastor Boone replied. "Moreover, he loves that which is part of you, and Helen loves him. You have seen his devotion to your daughter, to your whole family. He has put his uniform away. Ethan will burn it to appease you, he has told me so, and promised never to speak of the war in your presence. What more can you ask?"

The Colonel nodded at the missing hand.

"I've answered that," he said, "nothing more or less."

"Yes, you have, and in your family's presence," Pastor Boone said, allowing a terseness in his tone as well. "What about their wishes?"

"It was my hand taken and therefore my grievance, not theirs."

For a few moments the only sound was the fire's hiss and crackle.

"They could have married without your blessing," Pastor Boone said. "They can yet."

"Yes, and should they, let us be clear," the Colonel replied, "Helen will never step inside this house again, and if I see Ethan Burke on this land, or in town, or in church, I will kill him."

"You would need kill me too then, Father," Helen shouted from the porch.

Mrs. Davidson raised her hands to her ears.

"I will not listen to one word more," she said, her voice rising. "I will not. I will not."

When she turned to Pastor Boone, something seemed not so much to break inside her as wither. Mrs. Davidson's hands fell to her sides and her head drooped. For four years she had maintained the farm with her husband gone, no one to help but a daughter. Twice, outliers had come and stolen livestock, threatened to burn the house and barn down. Pastor Boone remembered how when the word came of Lee's surrender, no Confederate soldier's wife, including the woman before him, had mourned the lost cause. What tears had been shed were of relief it was finally over.

"There is no good in speaking of further violence," Pastor Boone said. "Haven't we all suffered enough these last years?"

"We, Pastor?" Colonel Davidson asked, his face reddening. "You dare speak to me of *your* suffering during the war.

"Fetch Pastor Boone's overcoat," the Colonel told his wife, and this time Mrs. Davidson did as she was told.

When Pastor Boone came outside, Ethan stood on the front step, Helen on the porch, their clasped hands bridging the boundary. They were arguing. Helen turned to Pastor Boone, tears in her eyes.

"Don't let Ethan do it."

"We shouldn't have bothered having you come," Ethan said. He freed his hands and gestured toward the axe. "It's the only thing to satisfy him. By God, I'll do it right now. I will."

Pastor Boone stepped close and took the youth by the elbow.

"You'll bleed to death or get gangrene. What good will come of that?"

"I've seen many a man live who lost an arm," Ethan said,

shaking free Pastor Boone's hand. "He in there survived it, didn't he?"

"Ride back with me," Pastor Boone said. "I promise we'll find a way, a way that won't risk your life."

"Listen to him, Ethan," Helen said. "Please."

"We've waited long enough," Ethan said, tears in his eyes as well now. "I've done all of everything else and it's still not enough."

"Just one more week," Pastor Boone said. "Allow me one week."

"Please, Ethan," Helen said, sobbing.

Ethan dried his eyes with a swipe of his forearm. He nodded and addressed the house.

"One week," the youth said loudly. "One week and I will do it, Colonel Davidson, I swear I will."

"I have always taken you for a wise man, William, despite your primitive beliefs," Doctor Andrews said the following morning. "But what you purpose is unworthy of a rational mind."

The two men sat in the house's back portion that served as office and examining room. Sickness, his or a congregant's, had brought Pastor Boone to this room many times, but more often it served as a salon for the best-educated men in Marshall to discuss everything from literature and politics to science and religion. The room had changed little in three decades. The Franklin clock ticked on the top bookshelf, beside it jars holding powders and tinctures. On the middle shelf was a solemn row of leather-spined medical books, below that *Man's Place in Nature* and *On the Origin of Species* set between volumes by Shakespeare, Scott, and Thackeray. The examining table pressed against the opposite wall; in the room's center sat a mahogany desk, one side bedecked with pill cutter, ledger, and mortaring pestle, the other a silver scale and balance aged to a dulled luster. An oil lamp sat on the desk, its flame alive. Because of the closed curtains, a lacquered darkness gave the office the aura of a confessional booth, which, like the room's seeming immutability, no doubt made it easier to speak of fears too often confirmed.

"There is no other way," Pastor Boone said. "Elopement is not possible and the Colonel's own wife and daughter cannot dissuade him. The youth has done all he can. For eight months, he's performed all manner of chores. Even in this weather, he was out there cutting and stacking wood. He offered to burn his uniform, and him on the winning side."

"The Colonel sounds rather like Prospero," Doctor Andrews said.

"Prospero forgave his enemies," Pastor Boone answered. "It was Ethan's notion to do the labors, and he's shown himself worthy of any man's daughter."

Doctor Andrews removed a briar pipe and tobacco box

from a drawer, as was his habit when anticipating a vigorous exchange. He tamped the tobacco and lit the pipe, doused the match with a sweep of the hand.

"I see that your new pipe has arrived."

"Yes," Doctor Andrews said, holding the briar pipe before them. "I only wish ideas could cross the ocean as quickly."

"So will you help us?"

"You have forgotten my oath, Pastor, *primum non nocere*."

"You will be healing, Noah, and not just two families but a whole community."

"But at such cost, William," Doctor Andrews replied. "They are young folks, both likable and attractive. If this union is not made, they will find others to betroth. With time, even accept that it was wise to do so."

"Ethan is resolute," Pastor Boone said. "What you will not do, he will do with an axe."

"You truly believe so?" Doctor Andrews asked. "My experience avers that, once the axe is in hand, such brash valor abates. At Bowman-Gray I saw my fellows swoon cutting cadavers. The same in this office. Men you would think fearless get the vapors seeing a few drops of blood."

"He saw blood and wounds in the war, no doubt amputations," Pastor Boone said. "If it's not done by someone else, he'll do it. He would have done so yesterday with the Colonel's own axe if I had not intervened. As for Leland

Davidson, you know the man. Do you believe he'd break a vow, any vow?"

"I do not," Doctor Andrews replied. "It would be an admission that he could be wrong."

The clock chimed on the half hour. Doctor Andrews set the pipe on the desk's spark-pocked wood.

"I must look in on Leah Blackburn. She has run a fever three days."

"You have proffered no answer," Pastor Boone said, but did not pause for one. "We are old men, Noah. Unlike the Colonel and this youth, we were spared the war's violence and suffering. Perhaps it's time for us to render what is our duty, even if we would wish it otherwise."

Doctor Andrews stood and Pastor Boone rose as well.

"Old men, William? Yes, I suppose we are," Doctor Andrews mused, rubbing his back. "I've watched others become gray and decrepit yet somehow presumed it was not happening to me. Is it so with you?"

"Sometimes," Pastor Boone answered.

"Perhaps it's because we are always looking for imperfections in others, and not ourselves," Doctor Andrews suggested.

"I've had cause to find plenty within myself," Pastor Boone said.

"If you mean your neutrality during the war, you protest too much, William. You did what you thought best, as did I."

"Best for the church or for myself?"

"Prudence was necessary," Doctor Andrews said. "I essayed no show of Unionist sympathies once the war began."

"But you did before. I did not even do that," Pastor Boone said. "Perhaps if I had, and done so forcefully, Leland Davidson would not have joined the Confederacy."

Doctor Andrews smiled.

"This present business should allay you of that vanity. Davidson is a man who values only his own opinion."

"But even now I don't understand his motivation to do so," Pastor Boone said. "He had no slaves to fight for."

Doctor Andrews set his pipe down.

"Perhaps I should not say this, William, but since you've broached the complexities of human motivation, might your involvement in this affair be of benefit to yourself as much as these young lovers?"

"In some ways, yes. I will admit that," Pastor Boone said, "but, as will be obvious, not in all."

"And you are certain he will sever his hand if I don't assent?" Doctor Andrews asked. "Absolutely certain?"

"Yes."

Doctor Andrews pressed his forehead with an open hand, as if to deflect some thought from breaking through.

"When would you have me do this?"

"Today," Pastor Boone replied. "Ethan said he'd wait a week, but I fear he won't wait that long."

"This afternoon at five o'clock then," Doctor Andrews said. "I visit my last patient at four, and I'll need to fetch Emma Triplett to assist me. But know I shall yet attempt to stop this folly. I will tell Ethan your motives are not solely in his interest, and point out that what seems brave and chivalrous today may not seem so when he has to support a family with one hand."

"No, not his hand," Pastor Boone said. "You have misconstrued my meaning."

The following afternoon the air still whitened each breath, but Pastor Boone and Ethan set out beneath a clear sky. The buggy passed slowly through town. Icicles dripped on posts and awnings, the thoroughfare a lather of mud and snow. Despite the cold, customers and storekeepers lined the boardwalks. Evelyn Norris, whose nephew had died in a Georgia prison camp, shook her head in dismay, but others tipped hats and nodded at Pastor Boone and Ethan. Several held out hands in the manner of a blessing. The Bible and package lay on the buggy seat between them, the rings set deep in Ethan's right pocket.

As they rode out of town, the slashes left by other wheels vanished. By the time they entered the woods, the only indentions were those of squirrels and rabbits. They passed over snapped limbs shackled with ice. A cardinal swung low and settled on a post oak branch.

"It always comes down to guilt, does it not, that and somebody's blood," Noah had said when he'd taken the ether from his cabinet. "Your religion, I mean."

Pastor Boone had been sitting on the operating table, shirt off, his eyes on the pieces of steel Emma Triplett had boiled and then set on a white towel. The woman had left the room and they were alone.

"I suppose, though I would add that hope is also a factor."

Doctor Andrews had grimaced.

"I can't believe I've allowed you to talk me into this barbarism, and for no other reason than some bundles of papyrus written thousands of years ago. We may as well be living in mud huts, grinding rocks to make fire. Huxley and his X Club will soon end such nonsense in England, but in this country we still believe the recidivists not the innovators bring advancement in human endeavors."

"I would say our country's military believe so," Pastor Boone answered as Emma Triplett came back in the room, "as evidenced by the number of deaths in this last conflict."

Emma Triplett handed a kerchief to the doctor, who nodded for Pastor Boone to lie down.

"Since a man of your advanced years may not rouse from this, I'll allow you the last word," Doctor Andrews said as he poured ether on the cloth, "although if you do pass on, and your metaphysics are correct, you shall quickly settle our debate once and for all."

Pastor Boone was about to speak of Mrs. Newell's similar doctrinal view, but the kerchief settled over his nose and mouth and the world wobbled a moment and then went black.

The woods thinned and the valley sprawled out before them. The Davidson farmhouse appeared and Ethan shook the reins to quicken the horse's pace. Pastor Boone's wrist throbbed, a vaguer ache where the hand had once been. The bottle of laudanum and a spoon were in his coat pocket, but if he took a dose, it would be just before the return to town. As the buggy jostled over the creek, Pastor Boone gasped.

"Sorry, Pastor," Ethan said. "I should have slowed the horse more."

"As long as you've waited," Pastor Boone replied, "a bit of haste is understandable."

A hound came off the porch, barked until it recognized Ethan. The buggy halted in front of the farmhouse and Ethan wrapped the check reins around the brake and jumped off. He helped Pastor Boone from the buggy's seat, being careful not to bump the bandaged wrist. The front door opened and Helen came out on the porch. Pastor Boone took the Bible off the seat.

"Bring the package," Pastor Boone said to Ethan, and stepped onto the porch.

"What happened, Pastor?" she asked, but then her face paled.

Ethan brought the package and Pastor Boone used his elbow and side to secure it.

"Stand behind me," he told them. "I'll call you when it's time to come inside."

Pastor Boone entered the parlor's muted light, set the Bible and package on the lamp stand. Mrs. Davidson offered to take the overcoat and he told her she'd have to help him. She held the overcoat in her hand, did not move to hang it up. Pastor Boone opened the Bible with his hand and found what he searched for. He left the Bible open and slipped two fingers between the pasteboard and the knot of twine. He lifted the package with the fingers in the manner of measuring its weight. He crossed the room to where the Colonel sat.

"I take you as a man of your word, Leland," Pastor Boone said, and set the package beside the Windsor chair. "Open it if you wish."

Pastor Boone went to the door and motioned Ethan and Helen inside. He took up the Bible and balanced it in his hand, positioned himself between the two young people.

"Mark 10, verse nine" Pastor Boone said. "*What therefore God hath joined together.*"

The Woman at the Pond

Water has its own archaeology, not a layering but a leveling, and thus is truer to our sense of the past, because what is memory but near and far events spread and smoothed beneath the present's surface. A green birthday candle that didn't expire with a wish lies next to a green Coleman lantern lit twelve years later. Chalky sun motes in a sixth-grade classroom harbor close to a university library's high window, a song on a staticky radio shoals against the same song at a hastily arranged wedding reception. This is what I think of when James Murray's daughter decides to drain the pond. A fear of lawsuits, she claims, something her late father considered himself exonerated from by posting a sign: FISH AND SWIM AT YOUR OWN RISK.

She hired Wallace Rudisell for the job, a task that requires opening the release valve on the standpipe, keeping it clear until what once was a creek will be a creek once more. I grew up with Wallace, and, unlike so many of our classmates, he and I still live in Lattimore. Wallace inherited our town's hardware store, one of the few remaining businesses.

"Bet you're wanting to get some of those lures back you lost in high school," Wallace says when I ask when he'll drain the pond. "There must be a lot of them. For a while you were out there most every evening."

Which is true. I was seventeen and in a town of three hundred, my days spent bagging groceries. Back then there was no internet, no cable TV or VCR, at least in our house. Some evenings that summer I'd listen to the radio or watch television with my parents, or look over college brochures and financial-aid forms the guidance counselor had given me, but I'd usually go down to the pond. Come fall of my senior year, though, Angie and I began dating. We found other things to do in the dark.

A few times Wallace or another friend joined me, but I usually fished alone. After a day at the grocery store, I didn't mind being away from people awhile, and the pond at twilight was a good place. The swimmers and other fishermen were gone, leaving behind beer and cola bottles, tangles of fishing line, gray cinder blocks used for seats. Later in the night, couples came to the pond, their leavings on the bank as well—rubbers and blankets, once a pair of panties hung on the white oak's limb. But that hour when day and night made their slow exchange, I had the pond to myself.

Over the years James Murray's jon-boat had become communal property. Having wearied of swimming out to retrieve the boat, I'd bought twenty feet of blue nylon rope to keep it moored. I'd unknot the rope from the white oak, set my fishing gear and Coleman lantern in the bow, and paddle out to the pond's center. I'd fish until it was neither day nor night, but balanced between. There never seemed to be a breeze, pond and shore equally smoothed. Just stillness, as though the world had taken a soft breath, and was holding it in, and even time had leveled out, moving neither forward nor back. Then the frogs and crickets waiting for full dark announced themselves, or a breeze came up and I again heard the slosh of water against land. Or, one night near the end of that summer, a truck rumbling toward the pond.

On Saturday I leave at two o'clock when the other shift manager comes in. I no longer live near the pond, but my mother does, so I pull out of the grocery store's parking lot and turn right, passing under Lattimore's one stoplight. On the left are four boarded-up stores, behind them like an anchored cloud, the mill's water tower, blue paint chipping off the tank. I drive by Glenn's Café where Angie works, soon after that the small clapboard house where she and our daughter, Rose, live. Angie's Ford Escort isn't there, but the truck belonging to Rose's boyfriend is. I don't turn in. It's not my weekend to be in charge, and at least I know Rose is on the pill, because I took her to the clinic myself.

Soon there are only farmhouses, most in disrepair—slumping barns and woodsheds, rusty tractors snared by kudzu and trumpet vines. I make a final right turn and park in front of my mother's house. She comes onto the porch and I know from her disappointed expression that she's gotten the week confused and expects to see Rose. We talk a minute and she goes back inside. I walk down the sloping land, straddle the sagging barbed wire, and make my way through brambles and broom sedge, what was once a pasture.

The night the truck came to the pond, an afternoon thunderstorm had rinsed the humidity from the air. The evening felt more like late September than mid-August. After rowing out, I had cast toward the willows on the far bank, where I'd caught bass in the past. The lure I used was a Rapala, my favorite because I could fish it on the surface or submerged. After a dozen tries nothing struck, so I paddled closer to the willows and cast into the cove where the creek ended. A small bass hit and I reeled it in, its red gills flaring as I freed the treble hook and lowered the fish back into the water.

A few minutes later the truck bumped down the dirt

road to the water's edge. The headlights slashed across the pond before the vehicle jerked right and halted beside the white oak as the headlights dimmed.

Music came from the truck's open windows and carried over the water with such clarity I recognized the song. The cab light came on and the music stopped. Minutes passed, and stars began filling the sky. As a thick-shouldered moon rimmed up over a ridge, a man and woman got out of the truck. The jon-boat drifted toward the willows and I let it, afraid any movement would give away my presence. The man and woman's voices rose, became angry, then a sound sharp as a rifle shot. The woman fell and the man got back in the cab. The headlights flared and the truck turned around, slinging mud before the tires gained traction. The truck swerved up the dirt road and out of sight.

The woman slowly lifted herself from the ground. She moved closer to the bank and sat on a cinder block. As more stars pierced the sky, and the moon lifted itself above the willow trees, I waited for the truck to return or the woman to leave, though I had no idea where she might go. The jon-boat drifted deeper into the willows, the drooping branches raking at my face. I didn't want to move, but the willows had entangled the boat. The graying wood creaked as it bumped against the bank. I lifted the paddle and pushed away as quietly as possible. As I did, the boat rocked and the metal tackle box banged against its side.

"Who's out there?" the woman asked. "I can see you, I can."

I lit the lantern and paddled to the pond's center.

"I'm fishing," I said, and lifted the rod and reel to prove it. The woman didn't respond. "Are you okay?"

"My face will be bruised," she said after a few moments. "But no teeth knocked out. Bruises fade. I'll be better off tomorrow than he will."

I set the paddle on my knees. In the quiet, it seemed the pond too was listening.

"You mean the man that hit you?"

"Yeah, him."

"Is he coming back?"

"Yeah, he's coming back. The bastard needs me to drive to Charlotte. Another DUI and he'll be pedaling to work on a bicycle. He won't get too drunk to remember that. Anyway, he didn't go far."

The woman pointed up the dirt road where a faint square of light hovered like foxfire.

"He's drinking the rest of his whiskey while some hillbilly whines on the radio about how hard life is. When the bottle's empty, he'll be back."

As the jon-boat drifted closer to the bank, the woman stood and I dug the paddle's wooden blade into the silt to keep some distance between us. The lantern's glow fell on both of us now. She was younger than I'd thought, maybe no more than thirty. A large woman, wide hipped and tall, at least five eight. Her long blond hair was clearly dyed. A red welt covered the left side of her face. She wore a man's leather jacket over her yellow blouse and black skirt. Mud grimed the yellow blouse. She raised her hand and fanned at the haze of insects.

"I hope there are fewer gnats and mosquitoes out there," she said. "The damn things are eating me alive."

"Only if I stay in the middle," I answered.

I glanced up at the truck.

"I guess I'll go back out."

I lifted the paddle, thinking if the man didn't come get her in a few minutes I'd beach the boat in the creek cove, work my way through the brush, and head home.

"Can I get in the boat with you?" the woman asked.

"I'm just going to make a couple of more casts," I answered. "I need to get back home."

"Just a few minutes," she said, and gave me a small smile, the hardness in her face and voice lessening. "I'm not going to hurt you. Just a few minutes. To get away from the bugs."

"Can you swim?"

"Yes," she said.

"What about that man that hit you?"

"He'll be there awhile yet. He drinks his whiskey slow."

The woman brushed some of the drying mud from her skirt, as if to make herself more presentable.

"Just a few minutes."

"Okay," I said, and rowed to the bank.

I steadied the jon-boat while she got in the front, the lantern at her feet. The woman talked while I paddled, not turning her head, as if addressing the pond.

"I finally get away from this county and that son of a bitch drags me back to visit his sister. She's not home so instead he buys a bottle of Wild Turkey and we end up here, with him wanting to lay down on the bank with just a horse blanket beneath us and the mud. When I tell him no way, he gets this jacket from the truck. For your head, he tells me, like that would change my mind. What a prince."

She shifted her body to face me.

"Nothing like coming back home, right?"

"You're from Lattimore?" I asked.

"No, but this county. Lawndale. You know where that is?"

"Yes."

"But our buddy in the truck used to live in Lattimore, so we're having a Cleveland County reunion tonight, assuming you aren't just visiting."

"I live here."

"Still in high school?"

I nodded.

"I'll be a senior."

"We used to kick your asses in football," she said. "That was supposed to be a big deal."

I pulled in the paddle when we reached the pond's center. The rod lay beside me, but I didn't pick it up. The lantern was still on, but we didn't really need it. The moon laid a silvery skim of light on the water.

"When you get back to Charlotte, will you call the police?"

"No, they wouldn't do anything. The bastard will pay though. He left more than his damn jacket on that blanket."

The woman took a wallet from the jacket, opened it to show no bills were inside.

"He got paid today so what he didn't spend on that whiskey is in my pocket now. He'll wake up tomorrow thinking a hangover is the worst thing he'll have to deal with, but he will soon learn different."

"What if he believes you took it?"

"I'll make myself scarce awhile. That's easy to do in a town big as Charlotte. Anyway, he'll be back living here before long."

"He tell you that?"

The woman smiled.

"He doesn't need to. Haven't you heard of women's intuition? Plus, he's always talking about this place. Badmouthing it a lot, but it's got its hooks in him. No, he'll move back, probably work at the mill, and he'll still be here when they pack the dirt over his coffin."

She'd paused and looked at me.

"What about you? Already got your job lined up after high school?"

"I'm going to college."

"College," she said, studying me closely. "I'd not have thought that. You've got the look of someone who'd stick around here."

Wallace waves from the opposite bank and makes his way around the pond. His pants and tennis shoes are daubed with mud. Wallace works mostly indoors, so the July sun has reddened his face and unsleeved arms. He nods at the valve.

"Damn thing's clogged up twice, but it's getting there."

The pond is a red-clay bowl, one-third full. In what was once the shallows, rusty beer cans and Styrofoam bait containers have emerged along with a ball cap and a flip-flop. Farther in, Christmas trees submerged for years are now visible, the black branches threaded with red-and-white bobbers and bream hooks, plastic worms and bass plugs, including a six-inch Rapala that I risk the slick mud to pull free. Its hooks are so rusty one breaks off.

"Let me see," Wallace says, and examines the lure.

"I used to fish with one like this," I tell him, "same size and model."

"Probably one of yours then," Wallace says, and offers the lure as if to confirm my ownership. "You want any of these others?"

"No, I don't even want that one."

"I'll take them then," Wallace says, lifting a yellow Jitterbug from a limb. "I hear people collect old plugs nowadays. They might be worth a few dollars, add to the hundred I'm getting to do this. These days I need every bit of money I can get."

We move under the big white oak and sit in its shade, watch the pond's slow contraction. More things emerge—a rod and reel, a metal bait bucket, more lures and hooks and bobbers. There are swirls in the water now, fish vainly searching for the upper levels of their world. A large bass leaps near the valve.

Wallace nods at a burlap sack.

"The bluegill will flush down that drain, but it looks like I'll get some good-sized fish to fry up."

We watch the water, soon a steady dimpling on the surface. Another bass flails upward, shimmers green and silver in the afternoon sun.

"Angie said Rose is trying to get loans so she can go to your alma mater next year," Wallace says.

"It's an alma mater only if you graduate," I reply.

Wallace picks up a stick, scrapes some mud off his shoes. He starts to speak, then hesitates, finally does speak.

"I always admired your taking responsibility like that. Coming back here, I mean." Wallace shakes his head. "We sure live in a different time. Hell, nowadays there's women who don't know or care who their baby's father is, much less expect him to marry her. And the men, they're worse. They act like it's nothing to them, don't even want to be a part of their own child's life."

When I don't reply, Wallace checks his watch.

"This is taking longer than I figured. I'm going to the café. I haven't had lunch. Want me to bring you back something?"

"A Coke would be nice," I say.

As Wallace drives away, I think of the woman letting her right hand brush the water as I rowed the jon-boat toward shore.

"It feels warm," she said, "warmer than the air. I bet you could slip in and sink and it would feel cozy as a warm blanket."

"The bottom's cold," I answered.

"If you got that deep," she said, "it wouldn't matter anyway, would it."

After we got out, the woman asked whose boat it was. I told her I didn't know and started to knot the rope to the white oak.

"Leave it untied then," she said. "I may take it back out."

"I don't think you should do that," I told her. "The boat could overturn or something."

"I won't overturn the boat," the woman said, and pulled a ten-dollar bill from her skirt pocket.

"Here's something for taking me out. This too," she said,

taking the jacket off. "It's a nice one and he's not getting it back. It looks like a good fit."

"I'd better not," I said, and picked up my fishing equipment and the lantern. I looked at her. "When he comes back, you're not afraid he'll do something else? I mean, I can call the police."

She shook her head.

"Don't do that. Like I said, he needs a driver, so he'll make nice. You go on home."

And so I did, and once there, did not call the police or tell my parents. I had trouble sleeping that night, but the next day at work, as the hours passed, I assured myself that if anything really bad had happened everyone in Lattimore would have known by now.

I went back to the pond, for the last time, that evening after work. The nylon rope was missing but the paddle lay under the front seat. As I got in, I lifted the paddle and found a ten-dollar bill beneath it. I rowed out to the center and tied on the Rapala and threw it at the pond's far bank.

As darkness descended, what had seemed certain earlier seemed less so. When a cast landed in some brush, I cranked the reel fast, hoping to avoid snagging the Rapala, but that also caused the lure to go deeper. The rod bowed and I was hung. Any other time, I'd have rowed to the snag and leaned over the gunwale, let my hand follow the line into the water to find the lure and free the hook. Instead, I tightened the line and gave a hard jerk. The lure stayed where it was.

For a minute I sat there. Something thrashed in the reeds, probably a bass or muskrat. Then the water was still. Moonlight brightened, as if trying to probe the dark water. I took out my pocketknife, cut the line, then rowed to shore and beached the boat. That night I dreamed that I'd let my hand follow the line until my fingers were tangled in hair.

Wallace's truck comes back down the dirt road. He hands me my Coke and opens a white bag containing his drink and hamburger. We sit under the tree.

"It's draining good now," he says.

The fish not inhaled by the drain are more visible, fins sharking the surface. A catfish that easily weighs five pounds wallows onto the bank as if hoping for some sudden evolution. Wallace quickly finishes his hamburger. He takes the burlap sack and walks into what's left of the pond. He hooks a finger through the catfish's gills and drops it into the sack.

In another half hour what thinning water remains boils with bass and catfish. More fish beach themselves and Wallace gathers them like fallen fruit, the sack punching and writhing in his grasp.

"You come over tonight," he says to me. "There'll be plenty."

As evening comes, more snags emerge, fewer lures. A whiskey bottle and another bait bucket, some cans that probably rolled and drifted into the pond's deep center. Then I see the cinder block, with what looks like a withered arm draped over it. Wallace continues to gather more fish, including a blue cat that will go ten pounds, its whiskers long as nightcrawlers. I walk onto the red slanting mud, moving slowly so I won't slip. I stop when I stand only a fishing rod's length from the cinder block.

"What do you see?" Walter asks.

I wait for the water to give me an answer, and before long it does. Not an arm but a leather jacket sleeve, tied to the block by a fray of blue nylon. I step into the water and loosen the jacket from the concrete, and as I do I remember the ten-dollar bill left in the boat, her assumption that I'd be the one to find it.

I feel something in the jacket's right pocket and pull out a withered billfold. Inside are two silted shreds of thin plastic, a driver's license, some other card now indiscernible. No bills.

I stand in the pond's center and toss the billfold's remnants into the drain. I drop the jacket and step back as Wallace gills the last fish abandoned by the water. Wallace knots the sack and lifts it. The veins in his bicep and forearm ridge up as he does so.

"That's at least fifty pounds' worth," he says, and sets the sack down. "Let me clear this drain one more time. Then I'm going home to cook these up."

Wallace leans over the drain and claws away the clumps of mud and wood. The remaining water gurgles down the pipe.

"I hate to see this pond go," he says. "I guess the older you get, the less you like any kind of change."

Wallace lifts the sack of fish and pulls it over his shoulder. We walk out of the pond as dusk comes on.

"You going to come over later?" he asks.

"Not tonight."

"Another time then," Wallace says. "Need a ride up to your mom's house?"

"No," I answer. "I'll walk it."

After Wallace drives off, I sit on the bank. Shadows deepen where the water was, making it appear that the pond has refilled. After a while I get up. By the time I'm over the barbed-wire fence, I can look back and no longer tell what was and what is.

Night Hawks

As she sat in the radio station's office, Ginny knew she could not have picked a better place to begin again. From midnight to six A.M., her main duty would be to slide disks into the beige CD player. Every fifteen minutes she would acknowledge requests, name artists and songs, and say pretty much anything to prove the music was not prerecorded.

"Research says almost ninety percent of people who listen from twelve to six are alone. It comforts them to know they're not the only person awake. Of course, that's what makes this job tough," Barry, the station manager, warned her at the interview. "The person you would replace claimed being alone here all night made him feel like the sole survivor of a nuclear holocaust. He was the third person I've hired in the last eighteen months. The solitude was harder on them than working nights."

During most of the interview, Barry had looked slightly above and to the left of Ginny, but now his eyes met hers.

"Coming from a school, you're used to a classroom full of kids."

"I've had plenty of experience with solitude," Ginny said, turning her face so he could see the scar more clearly.

As she drove home from the interview, Ginny passed the middle school where she'd taught. She slowed and saw Andrew's jeep in the parking lot, its back filled with poster boards and paints and brushes. Andrew was the county's middle-school art teacher and, for a time, Ginny's boyfriend. During her hospital stay, she'd thought things might have turned out different if Andrew had been at her school the afternoon of the accident. But she no longer believed that. She checked the dashboard clock, then looked up at the second-floor classroom that had been hers. The sixth graders would be back from lunch now, seated in their desks. They would be sleepy, harder to motivate, the adrenaline rush of morning recess long gone. This had been the slowest part of her school day.

Ginny had been more conscientious than most of her colleagues. While others merely glanced at assignments, she wrote detailed notes in the margins, adorned the pages with bright-colored stars and smiley faces. Every week she e-mailed parents about each child's progress. Once a month, she spent a Saturday morning creating a new motif for the bulletin board.

She'd had her failings as well. Dr. Jenkins, the principal, had noted on evaluations that some of her fellow teachers found her "aloof." Discipline had also been a problem. Two students whispering or a squabble at recess—each time Ginny felt her whole body tighten. Ginny usually could quell the misbehavior, but several times Dr. Jenkins had to come to restore order. But what had troubled Ginny the most, however, was the emotional distance between her and the students. She could not meet their obvious needs, even the boy with the purple birthmark splashed across his neck. She seemed unable to find the soothing words, know when to give the reassuring hug. Often she felt like an inmate pressing palm to glass and yet feeling no warmth from a hand less than an inch away.

No such distance had existed for Andrew on the Monday mornings she'd brought her class to the art room. His connection was evident as he moved from table to table, easel to easel, sometimes making suggestions but always finding something to praise. It was natural, instinctive. When he'd shown the class reproductions of famous paintings, his comments made each work seem created solely for the students.

Barry called the next morning and told her she had the job.

"When do I start?" she asked.

"I'm doing that shift myself now, so the sooner the better as far as I'm concerned. You can even start tonight if you want."

"What time should I be there?"

"Eleven. That'll give us an hour to go over what few bells and whistles we have, plus a chance for you to look over the CD library, get familiar with our board."

"Anything I need to do to prepare?"

"The best preparation is a lot of caffeine. Also, you'll need a moniker. There are kooks out there listening, especially late at night. Most are harmless, but not all. The less personal info you give the better."

"Anything else?" Ginny asked.

"The door will be locked when you get here. Knock loud so I can hear you."

Ginny found a notepad and pen. She'd written ten possible names before remembering the Edward Hopper painting Andrew had shown her students.

On her way to the radio station that night, Ginny slowed again as she passed the middle school. When she saw there was no fund-raiser or PTA meeting, she parked the car and stepped onto the school grounds for the first time since the accident. The moon was almost full, and its pale light revealed the clearance where the oak tree had been. She zipped her jacket but still shivered as she stood below the north wing, the oldest part of the building.

That day she'd heard the storm approach, thunder coming closer like artillery finding the range. The windows were at the back of the classroom, so she saw the oak limbs begin to sway. One night a week earlier a limb had broken a pane. The branches would be cut back soon, but until then Ginny was supposed to close the thick, plastic-backed drapes whenever a storm approached. But she had waited. David, her weakest student, was beside her desk, giving a report on Bolivia. Sheets of notebook paper quivered in his hands as he read with excruciating slowness. A student snickered when he read the same sentence twice. Other students, bored, quit paying attention. A balled-up piece of paper sailed across an aisle.

Stopping to close the drapes would only prolong the torment that was mercifully near its conclusion. But her concern was not just for David. If she stopped him now and went to the back of the room, she might lose complete control of the class. Spits of rain had begun to hit the glass. One of the oak tree's branches tapped a pane, demanding her attention. As David lost his place again, a student yawned loudly. The oak branch tapped the glass again, more insistent this time.

"I'm sorry, David," Ginny said, standing up from her desk. "I must stop you so I can close the drapes."

Amy Campbell, who sat on the row closest to the windows, stood as well.

"I'll close them, Miss Atwell," she said, and turned to the window.

"No, that's my job," Ginny said, just as a branch shattered the glass.

Amy had not fallen, had not even moved as glass shards flew around and into her. She had not made a sound. It was as if Amy had been asleep and it took the other children's screams to wake her. She had turned slowly toward Ginny. A glass shard was imbedded an inch below her right eye like a spear point.

Amy had reached up and pulled the shard from her face. For a moment there was no blood. As Ginny came toward her, Amy held the glass shard out as she might gum or some other middle-school contraband. Ginny took the piece of glass and with her free hand pressed a handkerchief against the wound.

The teacher next door ran into the room, soon followed by Dr. Jenkins, who took one look at the saturated handkerchief and told the other teacher to call 911. He and Ginny laid Amy on the floor. The child's eyes remained open but unfocused.

"She's in shock," Dr. Jenkins said.

He placed his jacket over Amy, then took the handkerchief's last dry corner and delicately probed the wound.

"Why weren't the drapes closed?" Dr. Jenkins asked.

Ginny said nothing and Dr. Jenkins turned his attention back to Amy. Another teacher herded the students out of the classroom and shut the door. For a few moments, all

Ginny had heard was a siren wailing through rain loud as a waterfall.

Dr. Jenkins would later claim that Ginny also had been in shock, because that was the only way to explain what Ginny had done next. As she kneeled beside Amy, Ginny opened the hand that held the glass shard.

"Be careful. That can cut you too," Dr. Jenkins warned.

But the words were hardly out of his mouth before Ginny raised the glass and jabbed its sharpest edge into her cheekbone. She'd moved the shard down her cheek to her mouth as deliberately as a man shaving.

Ginny had been drugged when Andrew came to her hospital room, but even drugged she could see how hard it was for him to look at her.

"You'll be all right," Andrew had said, holding her hand. "Dr. Jenkins has placed you on medical leave for the rest of the year. As soon as I'm out, we'll get away from here awhile, maybe Europe. Wherever you want to go, Ginny."

When she hadn't replied, Andrew had squeezed her hand.

"Rest," he said. "We can talk more about this later. We have a future."

But as she'd lain in the hospital bed that evening she thought not of the future but of the past. It had been in the sixth grade when Ginny quit raising her hand in class and began pressing her lips together during photographs. Her

permanent teeth had come in at angles that inspired nick-
names and jokes. Former friends no longer asked her to sit
with them at lunch. Ginny's father had been laid off at the
mill, making braces unaffordable. One late night her father
had awakened her, liquor on his breath as he told Ginny it
was a shitty world when a man couldn't prevent his own
daughter from being ashamed to smile.

Only her teachers had made life bearable, especially
Mrs. Ellison, her eighth-grade English teacher. She was the
one who'd convinced Ginny to be the student announcer on
the middle school's twice-weekly radio program. Once she
was out of sight behind the principal's microphone, Ginny
spoke without mumbling or covering her mouth. Mrs. Ellison praised how she never stumbled over words or rushed
her sentences. She said Ginny was a natural.

Late that spring Mrs. Ellison had cajoled an orthodontist
into working on Ginny's teeth for free. By the end of ninth
grade, she had no reason to turn her face from the world,
but certain habits had become ingrained. All through high
school, even into college, Ginny's hand gravitated to her upper lip as she spoke.

The habit of being alone was even harder to break, because solitude had its comforts. Most weekends she stayed
in her room, reading and listening to music, filling out scholarship and financial-aid forms. When Chapel Hill offered
Ginny a full academic scholarship, none of her teachers
were surprised. Several of them had, however, questioned

her decision to major in elementary education. As Ginny lay in the hospital bed, she knew they had been right.

When Dr. Jenkins visited the next morning, she told him that she would not return in the fall. Dr. Jenkins looked relieved. He wished Ginny well in whatever future path she undertook. Ending her relationship with Andrew had been more difficult. I need to be alone, she had told him. He had responded that she couldn't let the accident change what they had together. He'd spoken of love and devotion, of her moving in with him, of marriage. When he'd pleaded to at least be allowed to see her occasionally, she'd told him no. For several months he had tried anyway, calling nightly until she changed her cell number.

"This is the Night Hawk," Ginny said later that evening as the control booth clock ticked off the first seconds of the morning, "and I'll be with you till six. If you have a request, I'll do my best to play it for you. Just call 344-WMEK. Here's a song to get us started tonight."

Ginny hit the play button and the first notes of "After Midnight" filled the booth.

"Good choice," Barry said.

The next few hours went well. Barry helped her cue the advertisements and national news. He answered the phone for the occasional request. When she spoke into the microphone, she did little more than acknowledge a request or give the names of artists and songs she was about to play.

"I'm going home to get a few hours' sleep," Barry said after the three o'clock news. "Tom Freeman will be in around five thirty. He's got a key."

Barry pointed to a note card taped to the booth's one window.

"That's my home number. I'm only five minutes away. Call if you have a problem. But I don't think you'll need me. Except for getting comfortable enough to talk more, you've got this job down pat."

Ginny wasn't so sure, but after a few nights she did begin to talk more, though rarely about music. She brought in atlases and magazines, books that ranged from fat hardback tomes on western art to tattered paperback almanacs. Ginny quizzed her listeners twice an hour, rewarding those who answered correctly with WMEK T-shirts and ball caps. Each night she picked a word from *The Highly Selective Thesaurus for the Highly Literate* and gave its definition. She read from a book titled *On This Day in History*.

Some listeners called the station during business hours to complain about the new format, wanting less talk and more music. Several male listeners wanted some sports questions in Ginny's quizzes. But according to Barry, the calls and e-mails ran five to one in her favor, including several from immigrants who credited Ginny with teaching

them about American history. Two months later the Ar-
bitron ratings came out. WMEK's twelve-to-six slot had a
two-point market share increase.

"As long as you get that kind of response, I don't care
if you read the complete plays of William Shakespeare on
air," Barry told her.

It was a Thursday in early February when Andrew called.
Twelve inches of snow had fallen that day, and Barry, who
owned a truck, had to drive her to work. After reading cancellations for everything from schools to day-care centers to
shifts at local mills, she offered a free ball cap to a listener
naming the poem that began "Whose woods these are I
think I know."

There were two wrong answers before Andrew's voice
said, "Stopping by Woods on a Snowy Evening."

"You win a WMEK ball cap," Ginny said. "You can come
by the station during business hours to pick up your prize."

For several seconds neither spoke. Ginny cut the volume
in the control booth and heard the Norah Jones song she
was playing. She wondered if it was the radio in Andrew's
kitchen or the one in the back room where he painted.

"I knew you'd taken RTV classes, but I had no idea you
were doing this," Andrew said. "How long have you had the
job?"

"Almost three months."

"I just happened to have the radio on to find out about school cancellations."

"Well, it's a lucky night for you," Ginny said. "You've won a ball cap and no school tomorrow."

"The lucky thing is hearing your voice again," Andrew said. "I didn't realize how much I missed it until this last hour. Ten months haven't changed that. Don't you think it's time to let me back into your life?"

"I've got to go," Ginny said. "More cancellations to read."

Ginny hung up the phone. Only then did she realize her left hand was raised, her index finger touching her upper lip.

It was four hours later when she heard a banging on the door. Ginny cued another song and left the booth. She assumed it was Barry, but when she entered the foyer Andrew's face peered in through the glass. She kept the door latched.

"I've come to pick up my prize," he said, his breath whitened by the cold.

"The station doesn't open for business until eight thirty," Ginny said.

"You're here."

"I'm doing a program, a program I need to get back to."

"It's cold, Ginny. Let me come in."

She unlatched the door and he followed her to the control booth.

"You can sit over there," she said, pointing to a plastic chair in the corner.

Andrew watched and listened the next hour as she read cancellations, gave away another ball cap, and played several requests. Tom Freeman came in at 5:40 and Barry a few minutes later.

"This is the Night Hawk," Ginny said at 5:55, "and it's time to leave the airways to those birds that fly under the sun. So here's a song from those day-fliers The Eagles."

She turned up the volume as the intro to "Already Gone" filled the room.

"OK," she said to Andrew. "We can get your ball cap now."

Andrew followed her down the hall and into the station's reception room. Ginny opened a closet filled with ball caps and T-shirts.

"There," she said, handing him a cap. "Now you have what you came for."

"I wouldn't say that," Andrew said, fitting the cap on his head. "But it is a nice cap." He pulled the bill down slightly. "How does it look?"

"Perfect fit," Ginny said.

"I thought we might have breakfast together," Andrew said.

"Barry's supposed to take me home."

"I can take you home after we eat."

"I don't like to be around a bunch of strangers," Ginny said. "I get tired of the stares."

"We'll go where there aren't many people," Andrew answered. "That ought to be easy today. Everyone's hunkered down with their white bread and milk."

When she hesitated, Andrew placed his hand on her forearm.

"Please," Andrew said, "just breakfast."

"Let me tell Barry I'm going with you," Ginny said.

Soon they were driving through the center of town in Andrew's jeep. Few tire tracks marked the snow the jeep passed over.

"This should fit the bill nicely," Andrew said, and turned into the Blue Ridge Diner's parking lot.

The snow had stopped but gray clouds smothered the dawn. The parking lot lights were still on, casting a buttery sheen over the snow. Inside, the waitress and cook stood across the counter from a middle-aged couple who sat in plastic swivel chairs. They were talking about the weather, their voices soft as if also muffled by the snow.

"Let's sit in a booth," Ginny said.

The waitress turned from the others at the counter.

"You all want coffee?"

Andrew looked at Ginny and she shook her head.

"Just me," he said.

Andrew nodded toward the counter where the waitress continued to talk to the cook and the couple as she poured the coffee.

"A scene worthy of your moniker."

"No, not really," Ginny said. "Too much interaction."

Andrew turned his gaze back to her.

"In the painting the man and woman are a couple."

"I don't see that," Ginny said. "They aren't even looking at each other."

The waitress brought Andrew's coffee but no menus. When she saw Ginny's face up close, her lips pursed to an O before quickly turning to Andrew.

"There's not much choice as far as food," the waitress said. "Our deliveryman is running late, so it's pretty much waffles or jelly and toast."

"Waffles sound good," Andrew said.

Ginny nodded.

"Same for me."

Andrew stirred cream into his coffee. He held the cup but did not lift it to his lips. He leaned to blow across the coffee's surface, then raised his eyes.

"You're wrong about that couple in the painting."

"What do you mean?" Ginny asked.

"They are connected, the man and woman. Their faces may not show it but their arms and hands do."

"I don't remember that," Ginny said.

"Well, I'll show you then," Andrew said.

Coatless, he walked outside. Ginny watched through the window as he stepped into the lot, rummaged in the back of the jeep. The waitress brought their waffles.

Andrew returned with a gray hardback the width and thickness of a family Bible. He pushed his plate and cup to the side and laid the book open on the table.

"There," he said when he found the painting. "Look at her left arm and hand."

Ginny leaned over her plate and studied the picture.

"I'm not convinced. Because of the perspective it could go either way, like whether the Mona Lisa is smiling or not."

"Maybe you just don't want to admit you're wrong," Andrew said, and paused. "Maybe you're wrong about several things, like not being able to teach again, like you and me. . . ."

Andrew reached out and laid his palm against the scar on Ginny's face. She jerked her head sideways as if slapped.

"OK," he said, slowly lowering his hand. "I made a mistake tonight. It won't happen again."

They finished their waffles and coffee in silence, and did not speak until Andrew slowed in front of her apartment.

"Don't pull into the drive," Ginny said. "You might get stuck if you do."

Andrew pulled up to the curb but did not cut the engine.

Ginny got out and trudged across the yard, her black walking shoes disappearing in the white each time she took another step. She did not look back as she opened the front door. Inside, she took off her shoes and socks and brushed the snow off her pants. She looked out the window. Only one set of tracks crossed the yard. The jeep was gone.

——

Ginny slept as the sky cleared to a high, bright blue. By noon the temperature was in the forties. When her alarm clock went off at three, she lay in bed a few minutes listening to cars slosh through melting snow. She would not need a ride into work. She would drive herself across town, looking through safety glass as she passed the school where she had taught, then the hospital where her face had been stitched back together, the restaurant where she and Andrew had eaten breakfast.

At the radio station she would unlock the door, and soon enough Buddy Harper would end his broadcast and leave. She would say, *This is the Night Hawk*, and play "After Midnight." Ginny would speak to people in bedrooms, to clerks drenched in the fluorescent light of convenience stores, to millworkers driving back roads home after graveyard shifts. She would speak to the drunk and sober, the godly and the godless. All the while high above where she sat, the station's red beacon would pulse like a heart, as if giving bearings to all those in the dark adrift and alone.

Three A.M. and the Stars Were Out

Carson had gone to bed early, so when the cell phone rang he thought it might be his son or daughter calling to check on him, but as he turned to the night table the clock's green glow read 2:18, too late for a chat, or any kind of good news. He lifted the phone and heard Darnell Coe's voice. I got trouble with a calf that ain't of a mind to get born, Darnell told him.

Carson sat up on the mattress, settled his bare feet on the floor. Moments passed before he realized he was waiting for another body to do the same thing, leave the bed and fix him a thermos of coffee. Almost four months and it still happened, not just when he awoke but other times too. He'd read something and lower the newspaper, about to speak to an empty chair, or at the grocery store, reach into a shirt pocket for a neatly printed list that wasn't there.

He dressed and went out to the truck. All that would be needed lay in the pickup's lockbox or, just as likely, on Darnell's gun rack. At the edge of town, he stopped at Dobbins' Handy-Mart, the only store open. Music harsh as the fluorescent lights came from a counter radio. Carson filled the largest Styrofoam cup with coffee and paid Lloyd Dobbin's grandson. The road to Flag Pond was twenty miles of switchbacks and curves that ended just short of the Tennessee line. A voice on the radio said no rain until midday, so at least he'd not be contending with a slick road.

Carson had closed his office two years ago, referred his clients to Bobby Starnes, a new doc just out of vet school. Bobby had grown up in Madison County, and that helped a lot, but the older farmers, some Carson had known since childhood, kept calling him. Because they know you won't expect them to pay up front, or at all, Doris had claimed, which was true in some cases, but for others, like Darnell Coe, it wasn't. We've been hitched to the same wagon this long, we'll pull it the rest of the way together, Darnell had said, reminding Carson that in the 1950s and half a world away they'd made a vow to do so.

As the town's last streetlight slid off the rearview mirror, Carson turned the radio off. It was something he often did on late-night calls, making driving the good part, because what usually awaited him in a barn or pasture would not be good, a cow dying of milk fever or a horse with a gangrenous leg—things easily cured if a man hadn't wagered a vet fee against a roll of barbed wire or a salt lick. There had been times when Carson had told men to their faces they were stupid to wait so long. But even a smart farmer did stupid things when he'd been poor too long. He'd figure after a drought had withered his cornstalks, or maybe a hailstorm had beaten the life out of his tobacco allotment, that he was owed a bit of good luck, so he'd skimp on a calcium shot or pour turpentine on an infected limb. Waiting it out until he'd waited too late, then calling Carson when a rifle was the only remedy.

So driving had to be the good part, and it was. Carson had always been comfortable with solitude. As a boy, he'd loved to roam the woods, loved how quiet the woods could be. If deep enough in them, he wouldn't even hear the wind. But the best was afternoons in the barn. He'd climb up in the loft and lean back against a hay bale, then watch the sunlight begin to lean through the loft window, brightening the spilled straw. When the light was at its apex, the loft shimmered as though coated with a golden foil. Dust motes speckled the air like midges. The only sound would be underneath, a calf restless in a stall, a horse eating from a feed bag. Carson had always felt an aloneness in those moments, but never in a sad way.

Through the years, the same feeling had come back to

him on late nights as he drove out of town. Doris would be back in bed and the children asleep as he left the house. Night would gather around him, the only light his truck's twin beams probing the road ahead. He would pass darkened farmhouses and barns as he made his way toward the glow of lamp or porch light. On the way back was the better time, though. He'd savor the solitude, knowing that later when he opened the children's doors, he could watch them a few moments as they slept, then lie down himself as Doris turned or shifted so that some part of their bodies touched.

The road forked and Carson went right, passing a long-abandoned gas station. The cell phone lay on the passenger seat. Sometimes a farmer called and told Carson he might as well turn around, but this far from town the phone didn't work. The road snaked upward, nothing on the sides now but drop-offs and trees, an occasional white cross and a vase of wilted flowers. Teenage boys for the most part, Carson knew, too young to think it could happen to them. It was that way in war as well, until you watched enough boys your own age being zipped up in body bags.

Carson had been drafted by the army three months after Darnell joined the marines. They had not seen each other until the Seventh Infantry supported the First Marine at Chosin Reservoir, crossing paths in a Red Cross soup line. It was late afternoon and the temperature already below zero. The Chinese, some men claimed a million of them, were pouring in over the Korean border, and no amount of casualties looked to stop them. Let's make a vow to God and them Chinese too that if they let us get back to North Carolina alive we'll stay put and grow old together, Darnell had said. He'd held out his hand and Carson had taken it.

The road curved a final time, and the battered mailbox labeled COE appeared. Carson turned off the blacktop and bumped up the drive, wheels crunching over the chert rock. The porch light was on, from the barn mouth a lantern's lesser glow. Carson parked next to the unlatched pasture gate, got the medicine bag and canvas tool kit from the truck box. He shouldered the gate open and pushed it back. This far from town the stars were brighter, the sky wider, deeper. As on other such nights, Carson paused to take it in. A small consolation.

The lantern hung just inside the barn mouth, offering a thin apron of light to help Carson make his way. He took slow careful steps so as not to trip on old milking traces. At his age, he'd seen how one fall could end any sort of life worth living. Inside, it took a few moments to adjust to the barn's starless dark. Near the back stall, the cow lay on the straw floor. Darnell kneeled beside her, one hand stroking her flank. A stainless-steel bucket was close by, already filled with water, beside it rags and a frayed bedsheet. Darnell's shotgun, not his rifle, leaned across a stall door.

"How long?" Carson asked.

"Three hours."

Carson set the bags down and checked the cow's gums, then placed the stethoscope's silver bell against the flank before pulling on a shoulder glove.

"I think it's breeched," Darnell said.

Carson lubed the glove and slid his hand and forearm inside, felt a bent leg, then a shoulder, another leg, and, finally, the head. He slipped a finger inside the mouth and felt a suckle. Life stubbornly held on. Maybe he wouldn't have to pull the calf out one piece at a time. At least a chance.

"Not a full breech then," Darnell said when Carson pulled off the glove.

"Afraid it isn't."

Carson spread the tarp on the barn floor, set out what he'd need while Darnell retrieved the lantern and set it beside Carson. Inside the lantern's low light, the world shrank to a circle of straw, within it two old men, a cow, and, though curtained, a calf. Carson did a quick swab and pushed in the needle, waited for the lidocaine to ease the contractions. Darnell still stroked the cow's flank. As a young vet, Carson had quickly learned there were some men and women, good people otherwise, who'd let a lame calf linger days, not bothering to end its misery. They'd do the same with a sheep with blackleg. Never Darnell though. Because he'd witnessed enough suffering in Korea not to wish it on man or animal was what some folks would think, but Carson knew it to be as much Darnell's innate decency.

"Why the shotgun?" Carson asked.

"Coyotes. I've not heard any of late, but this is the sort of thing to draw them." Darnell nodded at the calf jack. "Figure you'll have to use it?"

"I'm going to try not to."

The cow's abdomen relaxed and the round eyes calmed. Somewhere in the loft a swallow stirred. Then the barn was silent and the lantern's light seemed to soften. The calf waited in its deeper darkness for Carson to birth it whole and alive or dead and in pieces. Carson's hands suddenly felt heavy, shackled. He looked down at them, the liver spots and stark blue veins, knuckles puffy with arthritis. He remembered another misaligned calf, not nearly as bad as this one. He was just months into his practice and had torn the cow's uterine wall, killing both cow and calf. Doris had been pregnant with their first child, and when she'd asked Carson if the calf and cow were okay, Carson had lied.

Darnell touched his shoulder.

"You all right?"

"Yeah."

Carson lubed his hand, no glove now, and slid it inside, pushed the calf as far back as he could, making space. Sweat trickled down his forehead, his eyes closed now to better imagine the calf's body. He found the snout, tugged it forward a bit, then back, and then to one side, and then another. Carson's heart banged his panting chest like a quickening hammer. The muscles in his neck and shoulder burned. He stopped for a minute, his arm still inside as he caught his breath.

"What do you think?" Darnell asked.

"Maybe," Carson answered.

Half an hour passed before he got the head aligned. Darnell gave him a wet hand cloth and Carson wiped the sweat off his face and neck. He rested a while longer before nodding at the tarp.

"Okay, let's get that leg."

Darnell hooked the OB chain to the handle and gave the other end to Carson, who looped the chain around a front leg. Darnell gripped the handle, and dug his boot heels into the barn floor.

"Okay," Carson said, his hand on the calf's leg.

The chain slowly tightened. Carson bent the foreleg to ensure the hoof didn't rake the uterine wall. Darnell did the hard work now, grunting as his muscles strained. They spoke little, Carson nodding left or right when needed. Minutes passed as the leg gave and caught. Like cracking a safe, that's how Carson thought of it, finding the combination that made the last tumbler fall into place. It felt like that, the womb swinging open and the calf withdrawn. There were times he could almost hear the click.

"Home free," Darnell gasped when the leg finally aligned.

Come morning, liniment would grease their lower backs and shoulders. They would move gingerly, new twinges and aches added to others gained over eight decades.

"Lord help us if our kids knew what we were up to to-night," Darnell said as he rubbed a shoulder. "They'd likely fix you and me up with those electronic ankle bracelets, keep us under house arrest."

"Which would show they've got more sense than we have," Carson replied.

The second leg took less than a minute and the calf slipped into a wider world. Carson cleared mucus from the snout, placed a finger inside the mouth and felt a tug.

"Much as we've done this, you'd think it might get a tad bit easier," Darnell said, "but that's not the way of it."

"No," Carson said. "Most things just get harder."

The last thing was calcium and antibiotic shots, but Carson doubted his hand capable of holding the needle steady. It could wait a few minutes. The men sat on the barn floor, weary arms crossed on raised knees as they waited for the calf to gain its legs. Carson leaned his head on his forearms and closed his eyes. He listened as the calf's hooves scattered straw, the body lifting and falling back until it figured out the physics. Once it did, Carson raised his head and watched the calf's knees wobble but hold. The cow was soon up too. The calf nuzzled and found a teat, began to suckle.

"There's a wonder to it yet," Darnell said, and Carson didn't disagree.

They watched a few more moments, not speaking. The lantern's wick burned low now. Carson resettled his hands, let his fingertips shift straw and touch the firmer earth as he leaned back. Only when the flame was a sinking flicker inside the glass did Darnell raise himself to one knee.

"Now let's see if we can get up too," he said.

Darnell grunted and stood, knees popping as he did so. He reached a hand under Carson's upper arm and helped him up, Carson's hinges grinding as well. Darnell lifted the lantern, turned the brass screw until light filled the globe again. He set the lantern down and walked over to the barn mouth, only his silhouette visible until a match rasped and illuminated his face a moment.

"So you're smoking again," Carson said.

"Nobody around to argue against it," Darnell answered. "Funny how you miss even the nagging."

"That's true," Carson said, and stepped over to the barn mouth and leaned against the opposite beam.

The stars sprawled yet overhead, though now Venus had tucked itself in among them. Though no more than a dozen feet apart, the men were mere shadows to each other. Carson watched the orange cigarette tip rise and hold a moment, then descend. A shifting came from the barn's depths, then a lapping sound as the cow's tongue washed the calf.

"Doris was a fine woman," Darnell said.

"Yes," Carson said, "she was."

"Four months now, ain't it?"

"Almost."

"It does ease up some, eventually," Darnell said.

He stubbed out his cigarette. Something between a sigh and a snicker crossed the dark between them.

"What's tickling your funny bone?" Carson asked.

"Just curious if the widows are showing up with their casseroles yet."

"No," Carson said. "I mean none since the funeral."

"Well, it won't be long and once it commences you'll think you're in the Pillsbury Bake-Off."

"I'm not looking for another wife," Carson said.

"I wasn't either but they came after me anyway. We're a rare commodity, partner. The one time I went down to that senior center, it was me and Ansel Turner and thirty blue-haired women. One of them decided we should have a dance. Soon as the music came on I got out of there and ain't been back, but poor old Ansel was in his wheelchair so couldn't get away. He was remarried in six months. They finally gave up on me but you're fresh game."

Darnell paused.

"I ain't making light of your loss."

"I know that," Carson said. "I've had plenty enough grieving words and hangdog faces. The sad part I don't need any help with."

He was rested enough now to give the shots, but waited. Except for speaking to his son and daughter on the phone, Carson hadn't much wanted to talk with people of late. But tonight, here in the dark with Darnell, there was a pleasure in it.

"The stars don't show out in town like they do here," Carson said.

"I'm not down there often of a night to know," Darnell answered, "but it's nice to look up and see something that never changes. When I was in Korea, I'd find the Big Dipper and the Huntress and the Archer. They hung in the sky different but I could make them out, same as if I was in North Carolina. There was a comfort in doing that, especially when the fighting got thick."

"I did that a couple of times too," Carson said.

Darnell lit another cigarette and stepped outside of the barn, listening until he was satisfied.

"They ain't yapping about it," Darnell said, "but they could still be out there."

Carson half stifled a yawn.

"I can put us on a pot of coffee."

"No," Carson answered. "I'll be on my way as soon as I give the shots."

"Back in Korea, we'd not have figured it to turn out this way, would we?" Darnell said. "I mean, we've gotten a lot more than we ever thought."

"Yes," Carson replied. "We have."

Carson went back inside, gave the shots, and packed up. Darnell lifted the lantern in one hand and the medicine bag in the other, led them back down to the pickup. Darnell opened his billfold and offered five ten-dollar bills that, as always, Carson refused. They shook hands and he got in the truck. As Carson bumped down the drive, he looked back and saw the lantern's glow moving toward the barn. Darnell would hang the lantern back on its nail, maybe smoke another cigarette as he stood at the barn mouth, attentive as any good sentry.